THE WAR
OF THE
WORLDS

SCHOLASTIC CLASSICS

THE WAR
OF THE
WORLDS

H.G. WELLS

With an introduction by Orson Scott Card

SCHOLASTIC INC.

New York   Toronto   London   Auckland   Sydney
Mexico City   New Delhi   Hong Kong   Buenos Aires

ISBN 0-439-80099-4

11 10 9 8 7 6 5 4 3 2 1   5 6 7 8 9/0

Printed in the U.S.A.   40

This edition first printing, September 2005

INTRODUCTION

When H.G. Wells wrote *The War of the Worlds*, science and technology had already changed much about the world, and promised to change even more.

Messages could be telegraphed wherever cable had been laid, and telephones allowed people to do business — or simply chat — with people who weren't in the same building.

The railroad had made transcontinental journeys almost routine, and steamships plied the oceans at speeds that would once have seemed miraculous.

Balloons took people higher than they had ever been able to go before, and using cameras the balloonists could take pictures of whole cities from the air. Gaslights illuminated the night and drove criminals back into the darkness.

Scientists and inventors seemed to be able to build whatever they could think of. The same power that ran the telephone and the telegraph might be used to record speech and music, or to light a room all night without gas. Inventors were working on carriages that could move without horses pulling them, and heavier-than-air flight, absurd as it sounded, was attracting many inventors, who risked life and limb to try out their contraptions.

Could it be that *anything* was possible? That *everything* was possible?

Relatively slight technological advantages had allowed Europeans to establish colonies on every continent. But after the industrial revolution, Europe was able to produce merchandise of such high quality and low price that they could trade with almost anyone — and those nations that resisted the European presence soon discovered the Europeans' advantage in weaponry.

It would be sixteen years before Europeans turned those weapons on each other in 1914 and nearly bled to death on the battlefields of France and Belgium. In 1898, that weaponry was still being used against ill-armed and badly organized natives or against colonials with no way to compete with the force the great European empires could bring to bear against them.

The great rush to colonize Africa was underway, with the imperial powers dividing the continent in arbitrary ways that would sow the seeds of chaos for a hundred years and more. It seemed, though, that wherever a European nation decided to establish its authority, it could sweep away all resistance the way someone might brush a spider off his arm.

H.G. Wells was certainly *not* predicting the future in *The War of the Worlds*. He was doing what he did best: telling a story that, by using fantastical ideas, forced its English-speaking readers to see the present — their own lives and nations — differently and perhaps more accurately.

After all, the one thing the British did not have to fear was invasion. The incomparable British navy ruled every ocean, and trade moved over the sea wherever the British wanted it to. No army could possibly reach the shores of Britain. Not for the British the experience of Africans, Indians, and East Asians, on whose shores strange white-skinned, round-eyed invaders appeared and showed that they could kill anyone from such a distance that they could barely be harmed by the local weapons of war.

So Wells brought strange, unexpected invaders from another world. In technology they were as much advanced over the English as the English were over their subjects in Africa and India. The readers of his story were forced to imagine their own cities falling before the mindless, devastating force of invaders who could not be bargained with or bought off. They didn't want human trade goods and they didn't respect human knowledge. They just wanted the land.

And then, suddenly, the threat evaporated.

Miraculous? Wish fulfillment? Was Wells saying, "Yes, I'll frighten you, but then I'll make it go away"?

Not really. Once again, he was simply taking a situation from the real world and twisting it a bit.

There was a very good reason why Africa had not been colonized years before. It wasn't for lack of trying, or because the Europeans hadn't yet "discovered" Africa.

For long centuries since the Portuguese had first sailed down the west coast of Africa to the habitable lands south of the Sahara, Europeans wanted to conquer the continent and take its riches. Instead, they were forced to do no more than buy slaves offered for sale by Africans along the coast, and in return sell the native peoples the rum and other trade goods they coveted.

Why no invasion?

Because Africa, the oldest home of the human race, had developed many endemic diseases that Africans had adapted to, but Europeans had not. The barrier of the Sahara desert had shielded the rest of the world from African diseases, because anyone who caught a disease south of the Sahara either got better or died by the time his caravan got back across the desert.

So when Europeans first tried to land and establish fortresses on the shores of sub-Saharan Africa, they were wiped out by plagues.

When you're dying of malaria, it's hard to make much use of your superior weapons to beat back attacks from angry Africans.

As a result, Europeans were forced to keep their distance from Africans who might transmit diseases. The Europeans built their fortresses on islands and rarely visited the populous lands ashore. Trade — even the slave trade — was conducted with as little direct contact as possible.

It was not until medicines like quinine made it possible for Europeans to survive malaria — and mosquito netting made it possible to avoid catching it in the first place — that the colonization of Africa became possible.

So disease served sub-Saharan Africa as an impregnable fortress for more than three centuries.

During that same period of time, all of the Americas had been utterly subjugated. The first colonies to win their independence were composed mostly of European immigrants, so that the level of technology was a near match. And nowhere were native Americans able to beat back the European assault.

That's because not only did the Europeans have superior technology, they also had the far more potent weapon of disease working in their favor. The very plagues that had once devastated Europe — most notably smallpox, but other diseases as well — spread as fast as rumor through the Americas, so that the conquistadors usually arrived in lands that had already lost half or three-quarters of their population to diseases to which the natives had no immunity.

So H.G. Wells was not writing about some remote, unimaginable future, or some fantastical universe in which impossible things might happen. He was writing about things that had already happened many times in fairly recent history.

The only important thing he changed about the story was that he put the shoe on the other foot: It was the world's only superpower, England, that was being invaded by technologically irresistible enemies, and it was not some secret weapon but rather a common, endemic disease that protected the natives from the alien invaders.

But this is how it usually is with science fiction.

Even though the term "science fiction" did not exist when Wells wrote his pivotal works, we who write and read science fiction follow in his footsteps, and the footsteps of Jules Verne. The first editor to create a magazine devoted to science fiction — Hugo Gernsback, who created *Amazing Stories* — stated outright that he wanted to publish a magazine that every month would be filled with stories like the "scientific romances" of H.G. Wells and the techno-adventures of Jules Verne.

Of course, most readers and many writers thought

they were writing about "the future." But even a little thought leads to the conclusion that there is no such thing as *the* future, only many possible futures. Only at the moment that the future becomes present does it get locked into a single track. And anyone who thinks he can guess, except in the broadest outlines, what the future will bring is doomed to disappointment or, if he was cocky enough about it, embarrassment.

To take some fairly recent examples, not one person in 1988 would have predicted that within the next two years, every eastern European nation would win its independence from the Soviet Union and would drive Communist governments out of power. Even if someone had dared to propose such a possibility, he would never have been foolish enough to suppose that the Soviet Union itself would break up and members of the Soviet Union like Ukraine, Belarus, and Moldova would become separate nations.

Yet all of this took place, and within an incredibly short period of time.

As it is with political and military history, so is it with technology. Isaac Asimov was fond of ruefully pointing out that while science fiction writers were quick to make use of computers in their fiction from the moment they were first put into operation in the days of Univac, nobody guessed how small they would become, so that science fiction from the 1940s and 1950s and even the 1960s often includes huge, building-sized computers. With the possible exception of the Dick Tracy comics, which foresaw miniaturization with devices like wristwatch radios that functioned like modern cell phones, nobody got the size right.

Nor will you find science fiction from the 1970s and 1980s that predicted the cell phone revolution and sharing of music over the Internet.

Does that mean science fiction writers "failed"? Not at all — even Wells has been shown to be "wrong" because Mars doesn't contain a dangerous, high-tech alien society.

Science fiction is not about the future. Like all other fiction, it is about the present. It simply uses different techniques to show us who we are, who we might be, and whom we ought to become.

Wells, a socialist, used *The Time Machine* to dazzle us with various science-inspired visions of the future, but the bulk of his story is devoted to a parable about English class struggle as seen through Fabian eyes: The powerful underclass, long exploited by the idle upper classes, had finally got its revenge by domesticating their one-time masters and harvesting them like cattle for food.

American science fiction, by contrast, seemed to miss the point and spent its efforts on stories that seemed to be about the science rather than the society. Look at these machines! How brilliantly they will change our lives! Or, when the writer was in a bad mood, Look at these machines! How quickly they can destroy us!

But even *those* stories were about the writers' own time and culture — for these American writers lived in a society that truly believed in progress. Just as science and technology were constantly advancing and improving, so the human race would also advance and improve, led by intrepid, resourceful, heroic but modest Americans.

Alvin York as played by Gary Cooper.

Science fiction, like all literature, reveals on every page the time and place it was written. What science fiction offers its authors and readers, from H.G. Wells and his audience to the present day, is clarity and surprise.

Real-world fiction presumably will surprise you less and less the better you know the real world. Science fiction, on the other hand, has the potential to surprise you by making unexpected changes in the reality of the story.

It's as if, in the midst of an intense family argument, one were led outside and forced to listen to the argument as a stranger might hear it. The sudden illumination is not always unpleasant, but it might actually make a difference to see ourselves in unexpected ways.

Naturally, as with every other literature, the repetitive soon came to predominate. Last year's surprises were recycled as the next year's "stories in the tradition of..." just as today you hear the echoes of Tolkien in most fantasy novels. It's hard to think of a theme of science fiction that was not anticipated by Wells and Verne.

Yet the best writers still find ways of using science fiction to illuminate the world we live in.

Why, though, is science fiction read so intensely by young people? Though there are many people who continue to read science fiction throughout their lives, a very large proportion of the genre's readers come to it young, read it intensely — sometimes exclusively — throughout junior high, high school, and college — and then never read it again. Why was it so important to them during their adolescence and early adulthood, only to be ignored later?

Of course, one could point out that it is precisely that age group that used to be the dominant readers of poetry and that most adults don't read anywhere near the quantity of literature they consumed in their youth. Nor do they read with the same intensity.

That is because youth is the age of Romance. Not boy-girl romance in the common meaning of the term, but rather the classical meaning of Romance: intense, passionate stories in which everything matters greatly. The hero is not just brave, he is the bravest; he does not save just himself, he saves the world. The poet is not merely somebody who happens to have a way with words; the poet sees the world through the eyes of genius and helps us understand the human condition. Everything the Romantic writer writes is bigger than life. Deeper, truer, richer, more brutal.

The fact is that there really are people in the world who are bigger than life. One thinks of Winston Churchill before World War II, repeatedly warning a pacifist world that Hitler was not going to stop until he had conquered the world and destroyed all the people he thought of as inferior.

But such people are rare. And they are never perfect. Churchill was prone to alcohol abuse and treated many of the people who worked for him quite callously. Yet few of them quit, for they understood that by putting up with him and helping him they might actually change the world for the better.

The fact is that human beings long for greatness. Even if they do not imagine that they are themselves capable of personal greatness, they long to be part of a great cause.

There is a reason why nations have always sent their young men off to war, rather than the old ones. It is the young men who are capable of believing in their cause so intensely that they will kill and die for it, casting away their lives in the service of something larger than themselves.

Youth is the age of poetry. And in our day, the literature that offers the visions of poetic greatness that young men and women long for is science fiction and fantasy.

Adolescence is the age when you cast off the role assigned to you by family and school and search for what you will be as an adult. No longer do you start with the assumption that you will follow in the footsteps of your parents and do whatever it was they did. You could be anybody, and could shape yourself and the world around you in a thousand different ways.

Science fiction offers youthful readers as many roles and as many worlds as they could hope for. When the writer's vision is bleak, the stories are bleaker than real life: The sun never shines, everyone is a power-hungry hypocrite, and only the hero maintains a spark of nobility in the midst of the cynicism. When the writer's vision is optimistic, the hero is at the cutting edge of a noble enterprise, willing to sacrifice himself to achieve great ends.

There isn't as much room for heroism in most other genres of literature. Yet the hunger for heroism is real: We need to know that what we're doing actually matters. And in Western culture, we have taken our young people and confined them in school during precisely the years when they are most hungry for greatness. Science fiction represents one avenue of escape from enforced meaninglessness.

So of course young readers are more drawn to science fiction than older ones. Science fiction shows them worlds that are far more fascinating and far more clear than the real world. Science fiction shows them heroes, demonstrating what nobility consists of to readers who have few real-world examples.

The fact that young readers embrace science fiction does not mean, however, that one *has* to "outgrow" it. Indeed, one might as easily say that those who leave science fiction behind them have not so much grown out of it as they have shrunk away from it. Having chosen their role in life and settled down to a career and a family, they no longer want infinite possibility and the dream of greatness; they want safety, predictability. And why shouldn't they?

But some people continue to hunger for the unpredictable experience, the taste of strangeness, and the hero whose vision or virtue might transform the world.

And some science fiction writers — the best, perhaps — are doing more with their fiction than satisfying the longings of youth. They are also doing their best to immunize their readers to the complacency of the "known world." However much adults might wish to live in a safe, predictable world, the fact is that they do not, and science fiction at its best is a constant reminder of that. Indeed, the very act of reading science fiction gives readers practical experience in adapting themselves to a world that is different from the ordinary one they think they live in. It gives us practice in coping with and adapting to unexpected change.

Martians will probably never invade Earth. But one might suppose that reading *The War of the Worlds* prepares its readers for experiences that do happen in the real world. Those who have lived in peace are never prepared for the sudden invasion by an enemy we did not suspect we had. But perhaps those who have read *The War of the Worlds* are better prepared for the possibility, less paralyzed when it comes — whether it comes in the form of German airplanes dropping bombs on London in World War II or terrorists crashing jets into buildings in twenty-first-century America.

Science fiction, then, presents the future — not by predicting it, but by preparing us to have the mental, emotional, and social skills to cope with change, with strangeness. It also prepares us for greatness — to know what the noble action might be, and to give us the courage to embrace it and carry it out. Who knows when and whether such skills will be needed?

And this branch of literature, with all that it offers, began with the writer whose book you now hold in your hands.

—Orson Scott Card

CONTENTS

Book I: *The Coming of the Martians*

Book II: *The Earth Under the Martians*

"*But who shall dwell in these worlds if they be inhabited? . . . Are we or they Lords of the World? . . . And how are all things made for man?*"—

KEPLER (*quoted in* The Anatomy of Melancholy).

THE WAR
OF THE
WORLDS

Book I
THE COMING
OF THE MARTIANS

1. The Eve of the War

No ONE would have believed in the last years
of the nineteenth century that this world was
being watched keenly and closely by intelligences greater than man's and yet as mortal
as his own; that as men busied themselves about
their various concerns they were scrutinized
and studied, perhaps almost as narrowly as a
man with a microscope might scrutinize the
transient creatures that swarm and multiply
in a drop of water. With infinite complacency
men went to and fro over this globe about
their little affairs, serene in their assurance of
their empire over matter. It is possible that the
infusoria under the the microscope do the same.
No one gave a thought to the older worlds of
space as sources of human danger, or thought

of them only to dismiss the idea of life upon them as impossible or improbable. It is curious to recall some of the mental habits of those departed days. At most, terrestrial men fancied there might be other men upon Mars, perhaps inferior to themselves and ready to welcome a missionary enterprise. Yet across the gulf of space, minds that are to our minds as ours are to those of the beasts that perish, intellects vast and cool and unsympathetic, regarded this earth with envious eyes, and slowly and surely drew their plans against us. And early in the twentieth century came the great disillusionment.

The planet Mars, I scarcely need remind the reader, revolves about the sun at a mean distance of 140,000,000 miles, and the light and heat it receives from the sun is barely half of that received by this world. It must be, if the nebular hypothesis has any truth, older than our world; and long before this earth ceased to be molten, life upon its surface must have begun its course. The fact that it is scarcely one seventh of the volume of the earth must have accelerated its cooling to the temperature at which life could begin. It has air and water and all that is necessary for the support of animated existence.

Yet so vain is man and so blinded by his vanity, that no writer, up to the very end of the nineteenth century, expressed any idea that intelligent life might have developed there far, or indeed at all, beyond its earthly level. Nor was it generally understood that since Mars is older than our earth, with scarcely a quarter of the superficial area and remoter from the sun, it necessarily follows that it is not only more distant from life's beginning but nearer its end.

The secular cooling that must some day overtake our planet has already gone far indeed with our neighbor. Its physical condition is still largely a mystery, but we know now that even in its equatorial region the midday temperature barely approaches that of our coldest winter. Its air is much more attenuated than ours, its oceans have shrunk until they cover but a third of its surface, and as its slow seasons change huge snowcaps gather and melt about either pole and periodically inundate its temperate zones. That last stage of exhaustion, which to us is still incredibly remote, has become a present-day problem for the inhabitants of Mars. The immediate pressure of necessity has brightened their intellects, enlarged their powers, and hardened their hearts. And looking across space with instruments, and intelligences such as we have scarcely dreamed of, they see, at its nearest distance only 35,000,000 of miles sunward of them, a morning star of hope, our own warmer planet, green with vegetation and gray with water, with a cloudy atmosphere eloquent of fertility, with glimpses

through its drifting cloud wisps of broad
stretches of populous country and narrow, navy-
crowded seas.

And we men, the creatures who inhabit this
earth, must be to them at least as alien and
lowly as are the monkeys and lemurs to us.
The intellectual side of man already admits
that life is an incessant struggle for existence,
and it would seem that this too is the belief of
the minds upon Mars. Their world is far gone
in its cooling and this world is still crowded
with life, but crowded only with what they regard as inferior animals. To carry warfare
sunward is, indeed, their only escape from the
destruction that generation after generation
creeps upon them.

And before we judge of them too harshly
we must remember what ruthless and utter destruction our own species has wrought, not only
upon animals, such as the vanished bison and
the dodo, but upon its own inferior races. The
Tasmanians, in spite of their human likeness,
were entirely swept out of existence in a war
of extermination waged by European immigrants, in the space of fifty years. Are we
such apostles of mercy as to complain if the
Martians warred in the same spirit?

The Martians seem to have calculated their
descent with amazing subtlety — their mathe-
matical learning is evidently far in excess of
ours — and to have carried out their prepara-

tions with a well-nigh perfect unanimity. Had our instruments permitted it, we might have seen the gathering trouble far back in the nine-teenth century. Men like Schiaparelli watched the red planet — it is odd, by-the-bye, that for countless centuries Mars has been the star of war — but failed to interpret the fluctuating appearances of the markings they mapped so well. All that time the Martians must have been getting ready.

During the opposition of 1894 a great light was seen on the illuminated part of the disk, first at the Lick Observatory, then by Perrotin of Nice, and then by other observers. English readers heard of it first in the issue of *Nature* dated August 2. I am inclined to think that this blaze may have been the casting of the huge gun, in the vast pit sunk into their plan-et, from which their shots were fired at us. Peculiar markings, as yet unexplained, were seen near the site of that outbreak during the next two oppositions.

The storm burst upon us six years ago now. As Mars approached opposition, Lavelle of Java set the wires of the astronomical exchange pal-pitating with the amazing intelligence of a huge outbreak of incandescent gas upon the planet. It had occurred toward midnight of the 12th; and the spectroscope, to which he had at once resorted, indicated a mass of flam-ing gas, chiefly hydrogen, moving with an

enormous velocity toward this earth. This jet
of fire had become invisible about a quarter
past twelve. He compared it to a colossal puff of
flame suddenly and violently squirted out of the
planet, "as flaming gases rushed out of a gun."

A singularly appropriate phrase it proved.
Yet the next day there was nothing of this in
the papers except a little note in the *Daily
Telegraph,* and the world went in ignorance
of one of the gravest dangers that ever threatened the human race. I might not have heard
of the eruption at all had I not met Ogilvy,
the well-known astronomer, at Ottershaw. He
was immensely excited at the news, and in the
excess of his feelings invited me up to take a
turn with him that night in a scrutiny of the
red planet.

In spite of all that has happened since, I still
remember that vigil very distinctly: the black
and silent observatory, the shadowed lantern
throwing a feeble glow upon the floor in the
corner, the steady ticking of the clockwork of
the telescope, the little slit in the roof — an
oblong profundity with the stardust streaked
across it. Ogilvy moved about, invisible, but
audible. Looking through the telescope, one saw
a circle of deep blue and the little round planet
swimming in the field. It seemed such a little
thing, so bright and small and still, faintly
marked with transverse stripes, and slightly
flattened from the perfect round. But so little it

was, so silvery warm — a pin's-head of light!
It was as if it quivered, but really this was
the telescope vibrating with the activity of the
clockwork that kept the planet in view.

As I watched, the planet seemed to grow
larger and smaller and to advance and recede,
but that was simply that my eye was tired.
Forty millions of miles it was from us — more
than forty millions of miles to void. Few people realize the immensity of vacancy in which
the dust of the material universe swims.

Near it in the field, I remember, were three
faint points of light, three telescopic stars infinitely remote, and all around it was the un-
fathomable darkness of empty space. You know
how that blackness looks on a frosty starlight
night. In a telescope it seems far profounder.
And invisible to me because it was so remote
and small, flying swiftly and steadily toward
me across that incredible distance, drawing
nearer every minute by so many thousands of
miles, came the Thing they were sending us,
the Thing that was to bring so much struggle
and calamity and death to the earth. I never
dreamed of it then as I watched; no one on
earth dreamed of that unerring missile.

That night, too, there was another jetting
out of gas from the distant planet. I saw it. A
reddish flash at the edge, the slightest projection, of the outline just as the chronometer
struck midnight; and at that I told Ogilvy and

he took my place. The night was warm and I
was thirsty, and I went, stretching my legs
clumsily and feeling my way in the darkness, to
the little table where the siphon stood, while
Ogilvy exclaimed at the streamer of gas that
came toward us.

That night another invisible missile started
on its way to the earth from Mars, just a second or so under twenty-four hours after the
first one. I remember how I sat on the table
there in the blackness, with patches of green
and crimson swimming before my eyes. I
wished I had a light to smoke by, little sus-
pecting the meaning of the minute gleam I
had seen and all that it would presently bring
me. Ogilvy watched till one, and then gave it
up; and we lit the lantern and walked over to
his house. Down below in the darkness were
Ottershaw and Chertsey and all their hundreds
of people, sleeping in peace.

He was full of speculation that night about
the condition of Mars, and scoffed at the vulgar
idea of its having inhabitants who were signaling us. His idea was that meteorites might
be falling in a heavy shower upon the planet,
or that a huge volcanic explosion was in progress. He pointed out to me how unlikely it
was that organic evolution had taken the same
direction in the two adjacent planets.

"The chances against anything manlike on
Mars are a million to one," he said.

Hundreds of observers saw the flame that night and the night after about midnight, and again the night after; and so for ten nights, a flame each night. Why the shots ceased after the tenth no one on earth has attempted to explain. It may be the gases of the firing caused the Martians inconvenience. Dense clouds of smoke or dust, visible through a powerful telescope on earth as little gray, fluctuating patches, spread through the clearness of the planet's atmosphere and obscured its more familiar features.

Even the daily papers woke up to the disturbances at last, and popular notes appeared here, there, and everywhere concerning the volcanoes upon Mars. The serio-comic periodical *Punch*, I remember, made a happy use of it in the political cartoon. And, all unsuspected, those missiles the Martians had fired at us drew earthward, rushing now at a pace of many miles a second through the empty gulf of space, hour by hour and day by day, nearer and nearer. It seems to me now almost incredibly wonderful that, with that swift fate hanging over us, men could go about their petty concerns as they did. I remember how jubilant Markham was at securing a new photograph of the planet for the illustrated paper he edited in those days. People in these latter times scarcely realize the abundance and enterprise of our nineteenth-century papers. For my own part, I was much occupied in learning to ride the bicycle, and busy upon a series of papers discussing the probable developments of moral ideas as civilization progressed.

One night (the first missile then could scarcely have been 10,000,000 miles away) I went for a walk with my wife. It was starlight, and I explained the signs of the zodiac to her, and pointed out Mars, a bright dot of light creeping zenithward, toward which so many telescopes were pointed. It was a warm night. Coming home, a party of excursionists from Chertsey or Isleworth passed us singing and playing music. There were lights in the upper windows of the houses as the people went to bed. From the railway station in the distance came the sound of shunting trains, ringing and rumbling, softened almost into melody by the distance. My wife pointed out to me the brightness of the red, green, and yellow signal lights hanging in a framework against the sky. It seemed so safe and tranquil.

2. The Falling Star

THEN CAME THE NIGHT of the first falling star. It was seen early in the morning rushing over Winchester eastward, a line of flame high in the atmosphere. Hundreds must have seen it, and taken it for an ordinary falling star. Albin described it as leaving a greenish streak behind it that glowed for some seconds. Denning, our greatest authority on meteorites, stated that the height of its first appearance was about ninety or one hundred miles. It seemed to him that it fell to earth about one hundred miles east of him.

I was at home at that hour and writing in my study; and although my French windows faced toward Ottershaw and the blind was up (for I loved in those days to look up at the

17

night sky), I saw nothing of it. Yet this strangest of all things that ever came to earth from outer space must have fallen while I was sitting there, visible to me had I only looked up as it passed. Some of those who saw its flight say it traveled with a hissing sound. I myself heard nothing of that. Many people in Berkshire, Surrey, and Middlesex must have seen the fall of it, and, at most, have thought that another meteorite had descended. No one seems to have troubled to look for the fallen mass that night.

But very early in the morning poor Ogilvy, who had seen the shooting star and who was persuaded that a meteorite lay somewhere on the common between Horsell, Ottershaw, and Woking, rose early with the idea of finding it. Find it he did, soon after dawn, and not far from the sand pits. An enormous hole had been made by the impact of the projectile, and the sand and gravel had been flung violently in every direction over the heath, forming heaps visible a mile and a half away. The heather was on fire eastward, and a thin blue smoke rose against the dawn.

The Thing itself lay almost entirely buried in sand, amidst the scattered splinters of a fir tree it had shivered to fragments in its descent. The uncovered part had the appearance of a huge cylinder, caked over and its outline softened by a thick scaly dun-colored incrustation. It had a diameter of about thirty yards. He approached the mass, surprised at the size and more so at the shape, since most meteorites are rounded more or less completely. It was, however, still so hot from its flight through the air as to forbid his near approach. A stirring noise within its cylinder he ascribed to the unequal cooling of its surface; for at that time it had not occurred to him that it might be hollow.

He remained standing at the edge of the pit that the Thing had made for itself, staring at its strange appearance, astonished chiefly at its unusual shape and color, and dimly perceiving even then some evidence of design in its arrival. The early morning was wonderfully still, and the sun, just clearing the pine trees toward Weybridge, was already warm. He did not remember hearing any birds that morning, there was certainly no breeze stirring, and the only sounds were the faint movements from within the cindery cylinder. He was all alone on the common.

Then suddenly he noticed with a start that some of the gray clinker, the ashy incrustation that covered the meteorite, was falling off the circular edge of the end. It was dropping off in flakes and raining down upon the sand. A large piece suddenly came off and fell with a sharp noise that brought his heart into his mouth.

For a minute he scarcely realized what this meant, and, although the heat was excessive, he clambered down into the pit close to the bulk to see the Thing more clearly. He fancied even then that the cooling of the body might account for this, but what disturbed that idea was the fact that the ash was falling only from the end of the cylinder.

And then he perceived that, very slowly, the circular top of the cylinder was rotating on its body. It was such a gradual movement that he discovered it only through noticing that a black mark that had been near him five minutes ago was now at the other side of the circumference. Even then he scarcely understood what this indicated, until he heard a muffled grating sound and saw the black mark jerk forward an inch or so. Then the thing came upon him in a flash. The cylinder was artificial — hollow — with an end that screwed out! Something within the cylinder was unscrewing the top!

"Good heavens!" said Ogilvy. "There's a man in it — men in it! Half roasted to death! Trying to escape!"

At once, with a quick mental leap, he linked the Thing with the flash upon Mars.

The thought of the confined creature was so dreadful to him that he forgot the heat, and went forward to the cylinder to help turn. But luckily the dull radiation arrested him before he could burn his hands on the still glowing metal. At that he stood irresolute for a moment, then turned, scrambled out of the pit, and set off running wildly into Woking. The time then must have been somewhere about six o'clock. He met a wagoner and tried to make him understand, but the tale he had told and his appearance were so wild — his hat had fallen off in the pit — that the man simply drove on. He was equally unsuccessful with the pot-man who was just unlocking the doors of the public house by Horsell Bridge. The fellow thought he was a lunatic at large and made an unsuccessful attempt to shut him into the tap-room. That sobered him a little; and when he saw Henderson, the London journalist, in his garden, he called over the palings and made himself understood.

"Henderson," he called, "you saw that shooting star last night?"

"Well?" said Henderson.

"It's out on Horsell Common now."

"Good Lord" said Henderson. "Fallen meteorite! That's good."

"But it's something more than a meteorite. It's a cylinder — an artificial cylinder, man! And there's something inside."

Henderson stood up with his spade in his hands.

"What's that?" he said. He was deaf in one ear.

Ogilvy told him all that he had seen. Henderson was a minute or so taking it in. Then he dropped his spade, snatched up his jacket, and came out into the road. The two men hurried back at once to the common, and found the cylinder still lying in the same position. But now the sounds inside had ceased, and a thin circle of bright metal showed between the top and the body of the cylinder. Air was either entering or escaping at the rim with a thin, sizzling sound.

They listened, rapped on the scaly burned metal with a stick, and, meeting with no response, they both concluded the man or men inside must be insensible or dead.

Of course the two were quite unable to do anything. They shouted consolation and promises, and went off back to the town again to get help. One can imagine them, covered with sand, excited and disordered, running up the little street in the bright sunlight just as the shop folks were taking down their shutters and people were opening their bedroom windows. Henderson went into the railway station at once, in order to telegraph the news to London. The newspaper articles had prepared men's minds for the reception of the idea.

By eight o'clock a number of boys and un-
employed men had already started for the
common to see the "dead men from Mars." That
was the form the story took. I heard of it first
from my newspaper boy about a quarter of
nine when I went out get my *Daily Chronicle*.
I was naturally startled, and lost no time in
going out and across the Ottershaw bridge to
the sand pits.

3. On Horsell Common

I FOUND A LITTLE CROWD of perhaps twenty people surrounding the huge hole in which the cylinder lay. I have already described the appearance of that colossal bulk, embedded in the ground. The turf and gravel about it seemed charred as if by a sudden explosion. No doubt its impact had caused a flash of fire. Henderson and Ogilvy were not there. I think they perceived that nothing was to be done for the present, and had gone away to breakfast at Henderson's house.

There were four or five boys sitting on the edge of the pit, with their feet dangling, and amusing themselves — until I stopped them — by throwing stones at the giant mass. After I had spoken to them about it, they began playing at "touch" in and out of the group of bystanders.

Among these were a couple of cyclists, a jobbing gardener I employed sometimes, a girl carrying a baby, Gregg the butcher and his little boy, and two or three loafers and golf caddies who were accustomed to hang about the railway station. There was very little talking. Few of the common people in England had anything but the vaguest astronomical ideas in those days. Most of them were staring quietly at the big tablelike end of the cylinder, which was still as Ogilvy and Henderson had left it. I fancy the popular expectation of a heap of charred corpses was disappointed at this inanimate bulk. Some went away while I was there, and other people came. I clambered into the pit and fancied I heard a faint movement under my feet. The top had certainly ceased to rotate.

It was only when I got thus close to it that the strangeness of this object was at all evident to me. At the first glance it was really no more exciting than an overturned carriage or a tree blown across the road. Not so much so, indeed. It looked like a rusty gas float. It required a certain amount of scientific education to perceive that the gray scale of the Thing was no common oxide, that the yellowish-white metal that gleamed in the crack between the lid and the cylinder had an unfamiliar hue. "Extraterrestrial" had no meaning for most of the onlookers.

At that time it was quite clear in my own mind that the Thing had come from the planet Mars, but I judged it improbable that it contained any living creature. I thought the unscrewing might be automatic. In spite of Ogilvy, I still believed that there were men in Mars. My mind ran fancifully on the possibilities of its containing manuscript, on the difficulties in translation that might arise, whether we should find coins and models in it, and so forth. Yet it was a little too large for assurance on this idea. I felt an impatience to see it opened. About eleven, as nothing seemed happening, I walked back, full of such thought, to my home in Maybury. But I found it difficult to get to work upon my abstract investigations.

In the afternoon the appearance of the common had altered very much. The early editions of the evening papers had startled London with enormous headlines:

"A MESSAGE RECEIVED FROM MARS"
"REMARKABLE STORY FROM WOKING"

and so forth. In addition, Ogilvy's wire to the Astronomical Exchange had roused every observatory in the three kingdoms.

There were half a dozen flys or more from

the Woking station standing in the road by the sand pits, a basket chaise from Chobham, and a rather lordly carriage. Besides that, there was quite a heap of bicycles. In addition, a large number of people must have walked, in spite of the heat of the day, from Woking and Chertsey, so that there was altogether quite a considerable crowd — one or two gaily dressed ladies among the others.

It was glaringly hot, not a cloud in the sky nor a breath of wind, and the only shadow was that of the few scattered pine trees. The burning heather had been extinguished, but the level ground toward Ottershaw was blackened as far as one could see, and still giving off vertical streamers of smoke. An enterprising sweet-stuff dealer in the Chobham Road had sent up his son with a barrow load of green apples and ginger beer.

Going to the edge of the pit, I found it occupied by a group of about half a dozen men — Henderson, Ogilvy, and a tall, fair-haired man that I afterward learned was Stent, the Astronomer Royal, with several workmen wielding spades and pickaxes. Stent was giving directions in a clear, high-pitched voice. He was standing on the cylinder, which was now evidently much cooler; his face was crimson and streaming with perspiration, and something seemed to have irritated him.

A large portion of the cylinder had been uncovered, though its lower end was still embedded.
As soon as Ogilvy saw me among the staring
crowd on the edge of the pit he called to me to
come down, and asked me if I would mind going
over to see Lord Hilton, the lord of the manor.

The growing crowd, he said, was becoming a
serious impediment to their excavations, especially the boys. They wanted a light railing put
up, and help to keep the people back. He told me
that a faint stirring was occasionally still audible within the case, but that the workmen had
failed to unscrew the top, as it afforded no grip
to them. The case appeared to be enormously
thick, and it was possible that the faint sounds
we heard represented a noisy tumult in the interior.

I was very glad to do as he asked, and so become one of the privileged spectators within the
contemplated enclosure. I failed to find Lord Hilton at his house, but I was told he was expected
from London by the six o'clock train from Waterloo; and as it was then about a quarter past
five, I went home, had some tea, and walked up
to the station to waylay him.

4. The Cylinder Opens

WHEN I RETURNED to the common the sun was setting. Scattered groups were hurrying from the direction of Woking, and one or two persons were returning. The crowd about the pit had increased, and stood out black against the lemon-yellow of the sky — a couple of hundred people, perhaps. There were raised voices, and some sort of struggle appeared to be going on about the pit. Strange imaginings passed through my mind. As I drew nearer I heard Stent's voice:

"Keep back! Keep back!"

A boy came running toward me.

"It's a-movin'," he said to me as he passed — "a-screwin' and a-screwin' out. I don't like it. I'm a-goin' 'ome, I am."

I went on to the crowd. There were really, I

29

should think, two or three hundred people el-
bowing and jostling one another, the one or two
ladies there being by no means the least active.

"He's fallen in the pit!" cried someone.

"Keep back!" said several.

The crowd swayed a little, and I elbowed my
way through. Everyone seemed greatly excited.
I heard a peculiar humming sound from the pit.

"I say!" said Ogilvy; "help keep these idiots
back. We don't know what's in the confounded
thing, you know!"

I saw a young man, a shop assistant in Woking I believe he was, standing on the cylinder
and trying to scramble out of the hole again. The
crowd had pushed him in.

The end of the cylinder was being screwed out
from within. Nearly two feet of shining screw
projected. Somebody blundered against me,
and I narrowly missed being pitched on to the
top of the screw. I turned, and as I did so the
screw must have come out, for the lid of the cylinder fell upon the gravel with a ringing concussion. I stuck my elbow into the person behind
me, and turned my head toward the Thing
again. For a moment that circular cavity seemed
perfectly black. I had the sunset in my eyes.

I think everyone expected to see a man
emerge — possibly something a little unlike us
terrestrial men, but in all essentials a man. I

know I did. But, looking, I presently saw something stirring within the shadow: grayish billowy movements, one above another, and then two luminous disks — like eyes. Then something resembling a little gray snake, about the thickness of a walking stick, coiled up out of the writhing middle, and wriggled in the air toward me — and then another.

A sudden chill came over me. There was a loud shriek from a woman behind. I half turned, keeping my eyes fixed upon the cylinder still, from which other tentacles were now projecting, and began pushing my way back from the edge of the pit. I saw astonishment giving place to horror on the faces of the people about me. I heard inarticulate exclamations on all sides. There was a general movement backward. I saw the shopman struggling still on the edge of the pit. I found myself alone, and saw the people on the other side of the pit running off, Stent among them. I looked again at the cylinder, and ungovernable terror gripped me. I stood petrified and staring.

A big grayish rounded bulk, the size, perhaps, of a bear, was rising slowly and painfully out of the cylinder. As it bulged up and caught the light, it glistened like wet leather.

Two large dark-colored eyes were regarding me steadfastly. The mass that framed them, the head of the thing, it was rounded, and had, one might say, a face. There was a mouth under the eyes, the lipless brim of which quivered and panted, and dropped saliva. The whole creature heaved and pulsated convulsively. A lank tentacular appendage gripped the edge of the cylinder, another swayed in the air.

Those who have never seen a living Martian can scarcely imagine the strange horror of its appearance. The peculiar V-shaped mouth with its pointed upper lip, the absence of brow ridges, the absence of a chin beneath the wedgelike lower lip, the incessant quivering of this mouth, the Gorgon groups of tentacles, the tumultuous breathing of the lungs in a strange atmosphere, the evident heaviness and painfulness of movement due to the greater gravitational energy of the earth — above all, the extraordinary intensity of the immense eyes — were at once vital, intense, inhuman, crippled, and monstrous. There was something fungoid in the oily brown skin, something in the clumsy deliberation of tedious movements unspeakably nasty. Even at this first encounter, this first glimpse, I was overcome with disgust and dread.

Suddenly the monster vanished. It had toppled over the brim of the cylinder and fallen into the pit, with a thud like the fall of a great mass of leather. I heard it give a peculiar thick cry, and forthwith another of these creatures appeared darkly in the deep shadow of the aperture.

I turned and, running madly, made for the first group of trees, perhaps a hundred yards away; but I ran slantingly and stumbling, for I could not avert my face from these things.

There, among some young pine trees and furze bushes, I stopped, panting, and waited further developments. The common round the sand pits was dotted with people, standing like myself in a half-fascinated terror, staring at these creatures, or rather at the heaped gravel at the edge of the pit in which they lay. And then, with a renewed horror, I saw a round, black object bobbing up and down on the edge of the pit. It was the head of the shopman who had fallen in, but showing as a little black object against the hot western sky. Now he got his shoulder and knee up, and again he seemed to slip back until only his head was visible. Suddenly he vanished, and I could have fancied a faint shriek had reached me. I had a momentary impulse to go back and help him that my fears overruled.

Everything was then quite invisible, hidden by the deep pit and the heap of sand that the fall of the cylinder had made. Anyone coming along the road from Chobham or Woking would

have been amazed at the sight — a dwindling
multitude of perhaps a hundred people or more
standing in a great irregular circle, in ditches,
behind bushes, behind gates and hedges, saying
little to one another and that in short, excited
shouts, and staring, staring hard at a few heaps
of sand. The barrow of ginger beer stood, a
queer derelict, black against the burning sky,
and in the sand pits was a row of deserted vehicles with their horses feeding out of nosebags
or pawing the ground.

5. The Heat Ray

AFTER THE GLIMPSE I had had of the Martians emerging from the cylinder in which they had come to the earth from their planet, a kind of fascination paralyzed my actions. I remained standing knee-deep in the heather, staring at the mound that hid them. I was a battleground of fear and curiosity.

I did not dare to go back toward the pit, but I felt a passionate longing to peer into it. I began walking, therefore, in a big curve, seeking some point of vantage and continually looking at the sand heaps that hid these newcomers to our earth. Once a leash of thin black whips, like the arms of an octopus, flashed across the sunset and was immediately withdrawn, and afterward a thin rod rose up, joint by joint, bearing

at its apex a circular disk that spun with a wob-
bling motion. What could be going on there?

Most of the spectators had gathered in one
or two groups — one a little crowd toward Woking, the other a knot of people in the direction
of Chobham. Evidently they shared my mental
conflict. There were few near me. One man I approached — he was, I perceived, a neighbor of
mine, though I did not know his name — and
accosted. But it was scarcely a time for articulate
conversation.

"What ugly *brutes!*" he said. "Good God!
what ugly brutes!" He repeated this over and
over again.

"Did you see a man in the pit?" I said; but he
made no answer to that. We became silent, and
stood watching for a time side by side, deriving,
I fancy, a certain comfort in each other's company. Then I shifted my position to a little knoll
that gave me the advantage of a yard or more
of elevation, and when I looked for him presently he was walking toward Woking.

The sunset faded to twilight before anything
further happened. The crowd far away on the
left, toward Woking, seemed to grow, and I
heard now a faint murmur from it. The little
knot of people toward Chobham dispersed.
There was scarcely an intimation of movement
from the pit.

It was this, as much as anything, that gave
people courage, and I suppose the new arrivals

from Woking also helped to restore confidence. At any rate, as the dusk came on a slow, intermittent movement upon the sand pits began, a movement that seemed to gather force as the stillness of the evening about the cylinder remained unbroken. Vertical black figures in twos and threes would advance, stop, watch, and advance again, spreading out as they did so in a thin irregular crescent that promised to enclose the pit in its attenuated horns. I, too, on my side began to move toward the pit.

Then I saw some cabmen and others had walked boldly into the sand pits, and heard the clatter of hoofs and the grind of wheels. I saw a lad trundling off the barrow of apples. And then, within thirty yards of the pit, advancing from the direction of Horsell, I noted a little black knot of men, the foremost of whom was waving a white flag.

This was the Deputation. There had been a hasty consultation, and since the Martians were evidently, in spite of their repulsive forms, intelligent creatures, it had been resolved to show them, by approaching them with signals, that we too were intelligent.

Flutter, flutter, went the flag, first to the right, then to the left. It was too far for me to recognize any one there, but afterward I learned that Ogilvy, Stent, and Henderson were with others in this attempt at communication. This little group had in its advance dragged inward, so to speak, the circumference of the now almost complete circle of people, and a number of dim black figures followed it at discreet distances.

Suddenly there was a flash of light, and a quantity of luminous greenish smoke came out of the pit in three distinct puffs, which drove up one after the other, straight into the still air.

This smoke (or flame, perhaps, would be the better word for it) was so bright that the deep blue sky overhead and the hazy stretches of brown common toward Chertsey, set with black pine trees, seemed to darken abruptly as these puffs arose, and to remain the darker after their dispersal. At the same time a faint hissing sound became audible.

Beyond the pit stood the little wedge of people with the white flag at its apex, arrested by these phenomena, a little knot of small vertical black shapes upon the black ground. As the green smoke arose, their faces flashed out pallid green, and faded again as it vanished. Then slowly the hissing passed into a humming, into a long, loud, droning noise. Slowly a humped shape rose out of the pit, and the ghost of a beam of light seemed to flicker out from it.

Forthwith flashes of actual flame, a bright glare leaping from one to another, sprang from the scattered group of men. It was as if some invisible jet impinged upon them and flashed into white flame. It was as if each man were suddenly and momentarily turned to fire.

Then, by the light of their own destruction, I saw them staggering and falling, and their supporters turning to run.

I stood staring, not as yet realizing that this was death leaping from man to man in that little distant crowd. All I felt was that it was something very strange. An almost noiseless and blinding flash of light, and a man fell headlong and lay still; and as the unseen shaft of heat passed over them, pine trees burst into fire, and every dry furze bush became with one dull thud a mass of flames. And far away toward Knaphill I saw the flashes of trees and hedges and wooden buildings suddenly set alight.

It was sweeping round swiftly and steadily, this flaming death, this invisible, inevitable sword of heat. I perceived it coming toward me by the flashing bushes it touched, and was too astounded and stupefied to stir. I heard the crackle of fire in the sand pits and the sudden squeal of a horse that was as suddenly stilled. Then it was as if an invisible yet intensely heated finger were drawn through the heather between me and the Martians, and all along a curving line beyond the sand pits the dark ground smoked and crackled. Something fell with a crash far away to the left where the road from Woking station opens out on the common.

Forthwith the hissing and humming ceased, and the black, domelike object sank slowly out of sight into the pit.

All this had happened with such switfness that I had stood motionless, dumbfounded and dazzled by the flashes of light. Had that death swept through a full circle, it must inevitably have slain me in my surprise. But it passed and spared me, and left the night about me suddenly dark and unfamiliar.

The undulating common seemed now dark almost to blackness, except where its roadways lay gray and pale under the deep-blue sky of the early night. It was dark, and suddenly void of men. Overhead the stars were mustering, and in the west the sky was still a pale, bright, almost greenish blue. The tops of the pine trees and the roofs of Horsell came out sharp and black against the western afterglow. The Martians and their appliances were altogether invisible, save for that thin mast upon which their restless mirror wobbled. Patches of bush and isolated trees here and there smoked and glowed still, and the houses toward Woking station were sending up spires of flame into the stillness of the evening air.

Nothing was changed save for that and a terrible astonishment. The little group of black specks with the flag of white had been swept out of existence, and the stillness of the evening, so it seemed to me, had scarcely been broken.

It came to me that I was upon this dark common, helpless, unprotected, and alone. Suddenly, like a thing falling upon me from without, came — fear.

With an effort I turned and began a stumbling run through the heather.

The fear I felt was no rational fear, but a panic terror not only of the Martians, but of the dusk and stillness all about me. Such an extraordinary effect in unmanning me it had that I ran weeping silently as a child might do. Once I had turned, I did not dare to look back.

I remember I felt an extraordinary persuasion that I was being played with, that presently, when I was upon the very verge of safety, this mysterious death — as swift as the passage of light — would leap after me from the pit about the cylinder and strike me down.

6. The Heat Ray in the Chobham Road

IT IS STILL a matter of wonder how the Martians are able to slay men so swiftly and so silently. Many think that in some way they are able to generate an intense heat in a chamber of practically absolute nonconductivity. This intense heat they project in a parallel beam against any object they choose by means of a polished parabolic mirror of unknown composition, much as the parabolic mirror of a lighthouse projects a beam of light. But no one has absolutely proved these details. However it is done, it is certain that a beam of heat is the essence of the matter. Heat, and invisible, instead of visible light. Whatever is combustible flashes into flame at its touch, lead runs like water, it softens iron, cracks and melts glass, and when it falls upon water, incontinently that explodes into steam.

That night nearly forty people lay under the starlight about the pit, charred and distorted beyond recognition, and all night long the common from Horsell to Maybury was deserted and brightly ablaze.

The news of the massacre probably reached Chobham, Woking, and Ottershaw about the same time. In Woking the shops had closed when the tragedy happened, and a number of people, shop people and so forth, attracted by the stories they had heard, were walking over the Horsell Bridge and along the road between the hedges that runs out at last upon the common. You may imagine the young people brushed up after the labors of the day, and making this novelty, as they would make any novelty, the excuse for walking together and enjoying a trivial flirtation. You may figure to yourself the hum of voices along the road in the gloaming....

As yet, of course, few people in Woking even knew that the cylinder had opened, though poor Henderson had sent a messenger on a bicycle to the post office with a special wire to an evening paper.

As these folks came out by twos and threes upon the open, they found little knots of people talking excitedly and peering at the spinning mirror over the sand pits, and the newcomers were, no doubt, soon infected by the excitement of the occasion.

By half-past eight, when the Deputation was destroyed, there may have been a crowd of three hundred people or more at this place, besides those who had left the road to approach the Martians nearer. There were three policemen too, one of whom was mounted, doing their best, under instructions from Stent, to keep the people back and deter them from approaching the cylinder. There was some booing from those more thoughtless and excitable souls to whom a crowd is always an occasion for noise and horseplay.

Stent and Ogilvy, anticipating some possibilities of a collision, had telegraphed from Horsell to the barracks as soon as the Martians emerged, for the help of a company of soldiers to protect these strange creatures from violence. After that they returned to lead that ill-fated advance. The description of their death, as it was seen by the crowd, tallies very closely with my own impressions: the three puffs of green smoke, the deep humming note, and the flashes of flame.

But that crowd of people had a far narrower escape than mine. Only the fact that a hummock of heathery sand intercepted the lower part of the Heat Ray saved them. Had the elevation of the parabolic mirror been a few yards higher, none could have lived to tell the tale. They saw the flashes and the men falling, and an invisible hand, as it were, lit the bushes as it hurried toward them through the twilight. Then, with a whistling note that rose above the droning of the pit, the beam swung close over their heads, lighting the tops of the beech trees that line the road, and splitting the bricks, smashing the windows, firing the window frames, and bringing down in crumbling ruin a portion of the gable of the house nearest the corner.

In the sudden thud, hiss, and glare of the igniting trees, the panic-stricken crowd seems to have swayed hesitatingly for some moments. Sparks and burning twigs began to fall into the road, and single leaves like puffs of flame. Hats and dresses caught fire. Then came a crying from the common. There were shrieks and shouts, and suddenly a mounted policeman came galloping through the confusion with his hands clasped over his head, screaming.

"They're coming!" a woman shirked, and incontinently everyone was turning and pushing at those behind, in order to clear their way to Woking again. They must have bolted as blindly as a flock of sheep. Where the road grows narrow and black between the high banks the crowd jammed, and a desperate struggle occurred. All that crowd did not escape; three persons at least, two women and a little boy, were crushed and trampled there, and left to die amid the terror and the darkness.

7. How I Reached Home

For my own part, I remember nothing of my flight except the stress of blundering against trees and stumbling through the heather. All about me gathered the invisible terrors of the Martians; that pitiless sword of heat seemed whirling to and fro, flourishing overhead before it descended and smote me out of life. I came into the road between the crossroads and Horsell, and ran along this to the crossroads.

At last I could go no farther; I was exhausted with the violence of my emotion and of my flight, and I staggered and fell by the wayside. That was near the bridge that crosses the canal by the gasworks. I fell and lay still.

I must have remained there some time.

I sat up, strangely perplexed. For a moment,

46

perhaps, I could not clearly understand how I came there. My terror had fallen from me like a garment. My hat had gone, and my collar had burst away from its fastener. A few minutes before there had only been three real things before me — the immensity of the night and space and nature, my own feebleness and anguish, and the near approach of death. Now it was as if something turned over, and the point of view altered abruptly. There was no sensible transition from one state of mind to the other. I was immediately the self of every day again — a decent, ordinary citizen. The silent common, the impulse of my flight, the starting flames, were as if they had been in a dream. I asked myself had these latter things indeed happened? I could not credit it.

I rose and walked unsteadily up the steep incline of the bridge. My mind was blank wonder. My muscles and nerves seemed drained of their strength. I dare say I staggered drunkenly. A head rose over the arch, and the figure of a workman carrying a basket appeared. Beside him ran a little boy. He passed me, wishing me good night. I was minded to speak to him, but did not. I answered his greeting with a meaningless mumble and went on over the bridge.

Over the Maybury arch a train, a billowing tumult of white, firelit smoke, and a long caterpillar of lighted windows, went flying south — clatter, clatter, clap, rap — and it had gone. A

dim group of people talked in the gate of one
of the houses in the pretty little row of gables
that was called Oriental Terrace. It was all so
real and so familiar. And that behind me! It
was frantic, fantastic! Such things, I told myself, could not be.

Perhaps I am a man of exceptional moods. I
do not know how far my experience is common.
At times I suffer from the strangest sense of
detachment from myself and the world about
me; I seem to watch it all from the outside,
from somewhere inconceivably remote, out of
time, out of space, out of the stress and tragedy
of it all. This feeling was very strong upon me
that night. Here was another side to my dream.

But the trouble was the blank incongruity of
this serenity and the swift death flying yonder,
not two miles away. There was a noise of business from the gasworks, and the electric lamps
were all alight. I stopped at the group of people.

"What news from the common?" said I.

There were two men and a woman at the gate.

"Eh?" said one of the men, turning.

"What news from the common?" I said

"Ain't yer just *been* there?" asked the men.

"People seem fair silly about the common,"
said the woman over the gate. "What's it all
abart?"

"Haven't you heard of the men from Mars?"
said I, "the creatures from Mars?"

"Quite enough," said the woman over the

gate. "Thenks." And all three of them laughed.

I felt foolish and angry. I tried and found I could not tell them what I had seen. They laughed again at my broken sentences.

"You'll hear more yet," I said, and went on to my home.

I startled my wife at the doorway, so haggard was I. I went into the dining room, sat down, drank some wine, and as soon as I could collect myself sufficiently I told her the things I had seen. The dinner, which was a cold one, had already been served, and remained neglected on the table while I told my story.

"There is one thing," I said, to allay the fears I had aroused — "they are the most sluggish things I ever saw crawl. They may keep the pit and kill people who come near them, but they cannot get out of it. . . . But the horror of them!"

"Don't, dear!" said my wife, knitting her brows and putting her hand on mine.

"Poor Ogilvy!" I said. "To think he may be lying dead there!"

My wife at least did not find my experience incredible. When I saw how deadly white her face was, I ceased abruptly.

"They may come here," she said again and again.

I pressed her to take wine, and tried to reassure her.

"They can scarcely move," I said.

I began to comfort her and myself by repeating all that Ogilvy had told me of the impossibility of the Martians establishing themselves on the earth. In particular I laid stress on the gravitational difficulty. On the surface of the earth the force of gravity is three times what it is on the surface of Mars. A Martian, therefore, would weigh three times more than on Mars, albeit his muscular strength would be the same. His own body would be a cape of lead to him. That, indeed, was the general opinion. Both *The Times* and the *Daily Telegraph*, for instance, insisted on it the next morning, and both overlooked, just as I did, two obvious modifying influences.

The atmosphere of the earth, we now know, contains far more oxygen or far less argon (whichever way one likes to put it) than does Mars. The invigorating influences of this excess of oxygen upon the Martians indisputably did much to counterbalance the increased weight of their bodies. And, in the second place, we all overlooked the fact that such mechanical intelligence as the Martians possessed was quite able to dispense with muscular exertion at a pinch.

But I did not consider these points at the time, and so my reasoning was dead against the chances of the invaders. With wine and food, confidence of my own table, and the necessity of reassuring my wife, I grew by insensible degrees courageous and secure.

"They have done a foolish thing," said I, fingering my wine glass. "They are dangerous because, no doubt, they are mad with terror. Perhaps they expected to find no living things — certainly no intelligent living things.

"A shell in the pit," said I, "if the worst comes to the worst, will kill them all."

The intense excitement of the events had no doubt left my perceptive powers in a state of erethism. I remember that dinner table with extraordinary vividness even now. My dear wife's sweet anxious face peering at me from under the pink lampshade, the white cloth with its silver and glass table furniture — for in those days even philosophical writers had many little luxuries — the crimson-purple wine in my glass, are photographically distinct. At the end of it I sat, tempering nuts with a cigarette, regretting Ogilvy's rashness, and denouncing the short-sighted timidity of the Martians.

So some respectable dodo in the Mauritius might have lorded it in his nest, and discussed the arrival of that shipful of pitiless sailors in want of animal food. "We will peck them to death tomorrow, my dear."

I did not know it, but that was the last civilized dinner I was to eat for very many strange and terrible days.

8. Friday Night

THE MOST EXTRAORDINARY THING to my mind, of all the strange and wonderful things that happened upon that Friday, was the dovetailing of the commonplace habits of our social order with the first beginnings of the series of events that was to topple that social order headlong. If on Friday night you had taken a pair of compasses and drawn a circle with a radius of five miles round the Woking sand pits, I doubt if you would have had one human being outside it, unless it were some relation of Stent or of the three or four cyclists or London people lying dead on the common, whose emotions or habits were at all affected by the newcomers. Many people had heard of the cylinder, of course, and talked about it in their leisure, but it certainly

did not make the sensation that an ultimatum
to Germany would have done.

In London that night poor Henderson's telegram describing the gradual unscrewing of the
shot was judged to be a canard, and his evening
paper, after wiring for authentication from him
and receiving no reply — the man was killed —
decided not to print a special edition.

Even within the five-mile circle the great majority of people were inert. I have already described the behavior of the men and women to
whom I spoke. All over the district people were
dining and supping; workingmen were gardening after the labors of the day, children were
being put to bed, young people were wandering
through the lanes lovemaking, students sat
over their books.

Maybe there was a murmur in the village
streets, a novel and dominant topic in the public houses, and here and there a messenger, or
even an eyewitness of the later occurrences,
caused a whirl of excitement, a shouting, and a
running to and fro; but for the most part the
daily routine of working, eating, drinking,
sleeping, went on as it had done for countless
years — as though no planet Mars existed in
the sky. Even at Woking station and Horsell
and Chobham that was the case.

In Woking junction, until a late hour, trains
were stopping and going on, others were shunting on the sidings, passengers were alighting

and waiting, and everything was proceeding in
the most ordinary way. A boy from the town,
trenching on Smith's monopoly, was selling papers with the afternoon's news. The ringing
impact of trucks, the sharp whistle of the engines from the junction, mingled with their
shouts of "Men from Mars!" Excited men came
into the station about nine o'clock with incredible tidings, and caused no more disturbance
than drunkards might have done. People rattling Londonward peered into the darkness
outside the carriage windows, and saw only a
rare, flickering, vanishing spark dance up from
the direction of Horsell, a red glow and a thin
veil of smoke driving across the stars, and
thought that nothing more serious than a heath
fire was happening. It was only round the edge
of the common that any disturbance was per-
ceptible. There were half a dozen villas burning
on the Woking border. There were lights in all
the houses on the common side of the three villages, and the people there kept awake till dawn.

A curious crowd lingered restlessly, people
coming and going but the crowd remaining, both
on the Chobham and Horsell bridges. One or two
adventurous souls, it was afterward found, went
into the darkness and crawled quite near the
Martians; but they never returned, for now
and again a lightray, like the beam of a warship's searchlight, swept the common, and the
Heat Ray was ready to follow. Save for such,

that big area of common was silent and desolate
and the charred bodies lay about on it all night
under the stars, and all the next day. A noise of
hammering from the pit was heard by many
people.

So you have the state of things on Friday
night. In the center, sticking into the skin of our
old planet Earth like a poisoned dart, was this
cylinder. But the poison was scarcely working
yet. Around it was a patch of silent common,
smoldering in places, and with a few dark,
dimly seen objects lying in contorted attitudes
here and there. Here and there was a burning
bush or tree. Beyond was a fringe of excitement,
and farther than that fringe the inflammation
had not crept as yet. In the rest of the world
the stream of life still flowed as it had flowed
for immemorial years. The fever of war that
would presently clog vein and artery, deaden
nerve and destroy brain, had still to develop.

All night long the Martians were hammering
and stirring, sleepless, indefatigable, at work
upon the machines they were making ready, and
ever and again a puff of greenish-white smoke
whirled up to the starlit sky.

About eleven a company of soldiers came
through Horsell, and deployed along the edge of
the common to form a cordon. Later a second
company marched through Chobham to deploy
on the north side of the common. Several officers from the Inkerman barracks had been on

the common earlier in the day, and one, Major
Eden, was reported to be missing. The colonel of
the regiment came to the Chobham bridge and
was busy questioning the crowd at midnight.
The military authorities were certainly alive to
the seriousness of the business. About eleven,
the next morning's paper were able to say, a
squadron of hussars, two Maxims, and about
four hundred men of the Cardigan regiment
started from Aldershot.

A few seconds after midnight the crowd in
the Chertsey road, Woking, saw a star fall from
heaven into the pine woods to the northwest. It
had a greenish color, and caused a silent brightness like summer lightning. This was the second cylinder.

9. The Fighting Begins

SATURDAY lives in my memory as a day of suspense. It was a day of lassitude too, hot and close, with, I am told, a rapidly fluctuating barometer. I had slept but little, though my wife had succeeded in sleeping, and I rose early. I went into my garden before breakfast and stood listening, but toward the common there was nothing stirring but a lark.

The milkman came as usual. I heard the rattle of his chariot, and I went round to the side gate to ask the latest news. He told me that during the night the Martians had been surrounded by troops, and that guns were expected. Then — a familiar, reassuring note — I heard a train running toward Woking.

"They aren't to be killed," said the milkman, "if that can possibly be avoided."

I saw my neighbor gardening, chatted with him for a time, and then strolled in to breakfast. It was a most unexceptional morning. My neighbor was of opinion that the troops would be able to capture or to destroy the Martians during the day.

"It's a pity that they make themselves so unapproachable," he said. "It would be curious to know how they live on another planet; we might learn a thing or two."

He came up to the fence and extended a handful of strawberries, for his gardening was as generous as it was enthusiatic. At the same time he told me of the burning of the pine woods about the Byfleet Golf Links.

"They say," said he, "that there's another of those blessed things fallen there — number two. But one's enough, surely. This lot'll cost the insurance people a pretty penny before everything's settled." He laughed with an air of the greatest good humor as he said this. The woods, he said, were still burning, and pointed out a haze of smoke to me. "They will be hot underfoot for days, on account of the thick soil of pine needles and turf," he said, and then grew serious over "poor Ogilvy."

After breakfast, instead of working, I decided to walk down toward the common. Under

the railway bridge I found a group of soldiers
— sappers, I think, men in small round caps,
dirty red jackets unbuttoned, and showing their
blue shirts, dark trousers, and boots coming to
the calf. They told me no one was allowed over
the canal, and, looking along the road toward
the bridge, I saw one of the Cardigan men standing sentinel there. I talked with these soldiers
for a time; I told them of my sight of the Martians on the previous evening. None of them
had seen the Martians, and they had but the
vaguest ideas of them, so that they plied me
with questions. They said that they did not
know who had authorized the movements of the
troops; their idea was that a dispute had arisen
at the Horse Guards. The ordinary sapper is a
great deal better educated than the common
soldier, and they discussed the peculiar conditions of the possible fight with some acuteness.
I described the Heat Ray to them, and they began to argue among themselves.

"Crawl up under cover and rush 'em, say I,"
said one.

"Get aht!" said another. "What's cover against
this 'ere 'eat? Sticks to cook yer! What we got
to do is go as near as the ground'll let us, and then
drive a trench."

"Blow yer trenches! You always want
trenches; you ought to ha' been born a rabbit,
Snippy."

"'Ain't they got any necks, then?" said a third, abruptly — a little, contemplative, dark man, smoking a pipe.

I repeated my description.

"Octopuses," said he, "that's what I calls 'em. Talk about fishers of men — fighters of fish it is this time!"

"It ain't no murder killing beasts like that," said the first speaker.

"Why not shell the darned things strite off and finish 'em?" said the little dark man. "You carn tell what they might do."

"Where's your shells?" said the first speaker. "There ain't no time. Do it in a rush, that's my tip, and do it at once."

So they discussed it. After a while I left them, and went on to the railway station to get as many morning papers as I could.

But I will not weary the reader with a description of that long morning and of the longer afternoon. I did not succeed in getting a glimpse of the common, for even Horsell and Chobham church towers were in the hands of the military authorities. The soldiers I addressed didn't know anything; the officers were mysterious as well as busy. I found people in town quite secure again in the presence of the military, and I heard for the first time from Marshall, the tobacconist, that his son was among the dead on the common. The soldiers had made the people

on the outskirts of Horsell lock up and leave
their houses.

I got back to lunch about two, very tired, for,
as I have said, the day was extremely hot and
dull; and in order to refresh myself I took a
cold bath in the afternoon. About half-past four
I went up to the railway station to get an evening paper, for the morning papers had contained only a very inaccurate description of the
killing of Stent, Henderson, Ogilvy, and the
others. But there was little I didn't know. The
Martians did not show an inch of themselves.
They seemed busy in their pit, and there was a
sound of hammering and an almost continuous
streamer of smoke. Apparently they were busy
getting ready for a struggle. "Fresh attempts
have been made to signal, but without success,"
was the stereotyped formula of the papers. A
sapper told me it was done by a man in a ditch
with a flag on a long pole. The Martians took as
much notice of such advances as we should of
the lowing of a cow.

I must confess the sight of all this armament,
all this preparation, greatly excited me. My
imagination became belligerent, and defeated
the invaders in a dozen striking ways; something of my schoolboy dreams of battle and
heroism came back. It hardly seemed a fair fight
to me at that time. They seemed very helpless
in that pit of theirs.

About three o'clock there began the thud of a gun at measured intervals from Chertsey or Addlestone. I learned that the smoldering pine wood into which the second cylinder had fallen was being shelled, in the hope of destroying that object before it opened. It was only about five, however, that a field gun reached Chobham for use against the first body of Martians.

About six in the evening, as I sat at tea with my wife in the summerhouse talking vigorously about the battle that was lowering upon us, I heard a muffled detonation from the common, and immediately after a gust of firing. Close on the heels of that came a violent, rattling crash quite close to us that shook the ground; and, starting out upon the lawn, I saw the tops of the trees about the Oriental College burst into smoky red flame, and the tower of the little church beside it slide down into ruin. The pinnacle of the mosque had vanished, and the roofline of the college itself looked as if a hundred-ton gun had been at work upon it. One of our chimneys cracked as if a shot had hit it, flew, and a piece of it came clattering down the tiles and made a heap of broken red fragments upon the flowerbed by my study window.

I and my wife stood amazed. Then I realized that the crest of Maybury Hill must be within the range of the Martians' Heat Ray now that the college was cleared out of the way.

At that I gripped my wife's arm, and without ceremony ran her out into the road. Then I fetched out the servant, telling her I would go upstairs myself for the box she was clamoring for.

"We can't possibly stay here," I said; and as I spoke the firing reopened for a moment upon the common.

"But where are we to go?" said my wife in terror.

I thought, perplexed. Then I remembered my cousins at Leatherhead.

"Leatherhead!" I shouted above the sudden noise.

She looked away from me downhill. The people were coming out of their houses astonished.

"How are we to get to Leatherhead?" she said.

Down the hill I saw a bevy of hussars ride under the railway bridge; three galloped through the open gates of the Oriental College; two others dismounted, and began running from house to house. The sun, shining through the smoke that drove up from the tops of the trees, seemed blood-red, and threw an unfamiliar lurid light upon everything.

"Stop here," said I; "you are safe here;" and I started off at once for the Spotted Dog, for I knew the landlord had a horse and dogcart. I ran, for I perceived that in a moment every one upon this side of the hill would be moving. I found him in his bar, quite unaware of what was going on behind his house. A man stood with his back to me, talking to him.

"I must have a pound," said the landlord, "and I've no one to drive it."

"I'll give you two," said I, over the stranger's shoulder.

"What for?"

"And I'll bring it back by midnight," I said.

"Lord!" said the landlord; "what's the hurry? I'm selling my bit of a pig. Two pounds, and you bring it back? What's going on now?"

I explained hastily that I had to leave my home, and so secured the dogcart. At the time it did not seem to me nearly so urgent that the landlord should leave his. I took care to have the cart there and then, drove it off down the road, and, leaving it in charge of my wife and servant, rushed into my house and packed a few valuables, such plate as we had, and so forth. The beech trees below the house were burning while I did this, and the palings up the road glowed red. While I was occupied in this way, one of the dismounted hussars came running up. He was going from house to house, warning people to leave. He was going on as I came out of my front door, lugging my treasures, done up in a tablecloth. I shouted after him:

"What news?"

He turned, stared, bawled something about "crawling out in a thing like a dish cover," and ran on to the gate of the house at the crest. A sudden whirl of black smoke driving across the road hid him for a moment. I ran to my neighbor's door and rapped to satisfy myself of what I already knew, that his wife had gone to London with him and had locked up their house. I went in again, according to my promise, to get my servant's box, lugged it out, clapped it beside her on the tail of the dogcart, and then caught the reins and jumped up into the driver's seat beside my wife. In another moment we were clear of the smoke and noise, and spanking down the opposite slope of Maybury Hill toward Old Woking.

In front was a quiet, sunny landscape, a wheatfield ahead on either side of the road, and the Maybury Inn with its swinging sign. I saw the doctor's cart ahead of me. At the bottom of the hill I turned my head to look at the hillside I was leaving. Thick streamers of black smoke shot with threads of red fire were driving up into the still air, and throwing dark shadows upon the green treetops eastward. The smoke already extended far away to the east and west — to the Byfleet pine woods eastward, and to Woking on the west. The road was dotted with people running toward us. And very faint now, but very distinct through the hot, quiet air, one heard the whirr of a machine gun that was presently stilled, and an intermittent cracking of rifles. Apparently the Martians were setting fire to everything within range of their Heat Ray.

I am not an expert driver, and I had immediately to turn my attention to the horse. When I looked back again the second hill had hidden the black smoke. I slashed the horse with the whip, and gave him a loose rein until Woking and Send lay between us and that quivering tumult. I overtook and passed the doctor between Woking and Send.

10. In the Storm

LEATHERHEAD is about twelve miles from Maybury Hill. The scent of hay was in the air through the lush meadows beyond Pyrford, and the hedges on either side were sweet and gay with multitudes of dog roses. The heavy firing that had broken out while we were driving down Maybury Hill ceased as abruptly as it began, leaving the evening very peaceful and still. We got to Leatherhead without misadventure about nine o'clock, and the horse had an hour's rest while I took supper with my cousins and commended my wife to their care.

My wife was curiously silent throughout the drive, and seemed oppressed with forebodings of evil. I talked to her reassuringly, pointing out that the Martians were tied to the pit by

sheer heaviness, and at the utmost could but
crawl a little out of it; but she answered only in
monosyllables. Had it not been for my promise
to the innkeeper, she would, I think, have urged
me to stay in Leatherhead that night. Would
that I had! Her face, I remember, was very
white as we parted.

For my own part, I had been feverishly excited all day. Something very like the war fever
that occasionally runs through a civilized com-
munity had got into my blood, and in my heart
I was not so very sorry that I had to return to
Maybury that night. I was even afraid that that
last fusillade I had heard might mean the extermination of our invaders from Mars. I can
best express my state of mind by saying that I
wanted to be in at the death.

It was nearly eleven when I started to return.
The night was unexpectedly dark; to me, walking out of the lighted passage of my cousins'
house, it seemed indeed black, and it was as hot
and close as the day. Overhead the clouds were
driving fast, albeit not a breath stirred the
shrubs about us. My cousins' man lit both lamps.
Happily, I knew the road intimately. My wife
stood in the light of the doorway, and watched
me until I jumped up into the dogcart. Then
abruptly she turned and went in, leaving my
cousins side by side wishing me good hap.

I was a little depressed at first with the contagion of my wife's fears, but very soon my

thoughts reverted to the Martians. At that time I was absolutely in the dark as to the course of the evening's fighting. I did not know even the circumstances that had precipitated the conflict. As I came through Ockham (for that was the way I returned, and not through Send and Old Woking) I saw along the western horizon a blood-red glow, which, as I drew nearer, crept slowly up the sky. The driving clouds of the gathering thunderstorm mingled there with masses of black and red smoke.

Ripley Street was deserted, and except for a lighted window or so the village showed not a sign of life; but I narrowly escaped an accident at the corner of the road to Pyrford, where a knot of people stood with their backs to me. They said nothing to me as I passed. I do not know what they knew of the things happening beyond the hill, nor do I know if the silent houses I passed on my way were sleeping securely, or deserted and empty, or harassed and watching against the terror of the night.

From Ripley until I came through Pyrford I was in the valley of the Wey, and the red glare was hidden from me. As I ascended the little hill beyond Pyrford Church the glare came into view again, and the trees about me shivered with the first intimation of the storm that was upon me. Then I heard midnight pealing out from Pyrford Church behind me, and then came the silhouette of Maybury Hill, with its treetops and roofs black and sharp against the red.

Even as I beheld this a lurid green glare lit the road about me and showed the distant woods toward Addlestone. I felt a tug at the reins. I saw that the driving clouds had been pierced as it were by a thread of green fire, suddenly lighting their confusion and falling into the field to my left. It was the Third Falling Star!

Close on its apparition, and blindingly violet by contrast, danced out the first lightning of the gathering storm, and the thunder burst like a rocket overhead. The horse took the bit between his teeth and bolted.

A moderate incline runs toward the foot of Maybury Hill, and down this we clattered. Once the lightning had begun, it went on in as rapid a succession of flashes as I have ever seen. The thunderclaps, treading one on the heels of another and with a strange crackling accompaniment, sounded more like the working of a gigantic electric machine than the usual detonating reverberations. The flickering light was blinding and confusing, and a thin hail smote gustily at my face as I drove down the slope.

At first I regarded little but the road before me, and then abruptly my attention was arrested by something that was moving rapidly down the opposite slope of Maybury Hill. At first I took it for the wet roof of a house, but one flash following another showed it to be in swift rolling movement. It was an elusive vision — a moment of bewildering darkness, and then, in a flash like daylight, the red masses of the orphanage near the crest of the hill, the green tops of the pine trees, and this problematical object came out clear and sharp and bright.

And this Thing I saw! How can I describe it? A monstrous tripod, higher than many houses, striding over the young pine trees, and smashing them aside in its career; a walking engine of glittering metal, striding now across the heather; articulate ropes of steel dangling from it, and the clattering tumult of its passage mingling with the riot of the thunder. A flash, and it came out vividly, heeling over one way with two feet in the air, to vanish and reappear almost instantly as it seemed, with the next flash, a hundred yards nearer. Can you imagine a milking stool tilted and bowled violently along the ground? That was the impression those instant flashes gave. But instead of a milking stool imagine it a great body of machinery on a tripod stand.

Then suddenly the trees in the pine wood ahead of me were parted, as brittle reeds are parted by a man thrusting through them; they were snapped off and driven headlong, and a second huge tripod appeared, rushing, as it seemed, headlong toward me. And I was galloping hard to meet it! At the sight of the second monster my nerve went altogether. Not stopping to look again, I wrenched the horse's head

hard round to the right, and in another moment
the dogcart had heeled over upon the horse;
the shafts smashed noisily, and I was flung sideways and fell heavily into a shallow pool of
water.

I crawled out almost immediately, and
crouched, my feet still in the water, under a
clump of furze. The horse lay motionless (his
neck was broken, poor brute!) and by the
lightning flashes I saw the black bulk of the
overturned dogcart and the silhouette of the
wheel still spinning slowly. In another moment
the colossal mechanism went striding by me,
and passed uphill toward Pyrford.

Seen nearer, the Thing was incredibly
strange, for it was no mere insensate machine
driving on its way. Machine it was, with a
ringing metallic pace, and long, flexible, glittering tentacles (one of which gripped a young pine
tree) swinging and rattling about its strange
body. It picked its road as it went striding
along, and the brazen hood that surmounted it
moved to and fro with the inevitable suggestion
of a head looking about. Behind the main body
was a huge mass of white metal like a gigantic
fisherman's basket, and puffs of green smoke
squirted out from the joints of the limbs as the
monster swept by me. And in an instant it was
gone.

So much I saw then, all vaguely for the flickering of the lightning, in blinding high lights and dense black shadows.

As it passed it set up an exultant deafening howl that drowned the thunder — "Aloo! aloo!" — and in another minute it was with its companion, half a mile away, stooping over something in the field. I have no doubt this Thing in the field was the third of the ten cylinders they had fired at us from Mars.

For some minutes I lay there in the rain and darkness watching, by the intermittent light, these monstrous beings of metal moving about in the distance over the hedge tops. A thin hail was now beginning, and as it came and went their figures grew misty and then flashed into clearness again. Now and then came a gap in the lightning, and the night swallowed them up.

I was soaked with hail above and puddle water below. It was some time before my blank astonishment would let me struggle up the bank to a drier position, or think at all of my imminent peril.

Not far from me was a little one-room squatter's hut of wood, surrounded by a patch of potato garden. I struggled to my feet at last, and, crouching and making use of every chance of cover, I made a run for this. I hammered at the door, but I could not make the people hear (if there were any people inside), and after a time I desisted, and, availing myself of a ditch for the greater part of the way, succeeded in crawling, unobserved by these monstrous machines, into the pine wood toward Maybury.

Under cover of this I pushed on, wet and shivering now, toward my own house. I walked among the trees trying to find the footpatch. It was very dark indeed in the wood, for the lightning was now becoming infrequent, and the hail, which was pouring down in a torrent, fell in columns through the gaps in the heavy foliage.

If I had fully realized the meaning of all the things I had seen I should have immediately worked my way round through Byfleet to Street Cobham, and so gone back to rejoin my wife at Leatherhead. But that night the strangeness of things about me, and my physical wretchedness, prevented me, for I was bruised, weary, wet to the skin, deafened and blinded by the storm.

I had a vague idea of going on to my own house, and that was as much motive as I had. I staggered through the trees, fell into a ditch and bruised my knees against a plank, and finally splashed out into the lane that ran down from the College Arms. I say splashed, for the storm water was sweeping the sand down the hill in a muddy torrent. There in the darkness a man blundered into me and sent me reeling back.

He gave a cry of terror, sprang sideways, and rushed on before I could gather my wits suffi-

ciently to speak to him. So heavy was the stress
of the storm just at this place that I had the
hardest task to win my way up the hill. I went
close up to the fence on the left and worked my
way along its palings.

Near the top I stumbled upon something soft,
and, by a flash of lightning, saw between my
feet a heap of black broadcloth and a pair of
boots. Before I could distinguish clearly how the
man lay, the flicker of light had passed. I stood
over him waiting for the next flash. When it
came, I saw that he was a sturdy man, cheaply
but not shabbily dressed; his head was bent under his body, and he lay crumpled up close to the
fence, as though he had been flung violently
against it.

Overcoming the repugnance natural to one
who had never before touched a dead body, I
stooped and turned him over to feel for his
heart. He was quite dead. Apparently his neck
had been broken. The lightning flashed for a
third time, and his face leaped upon me. I
sprang to my feet. It was the landlord of the
Spotted Dog, whose conveyance I had taken.

I stepped over him gingerly and pushed on
up the hill. I made my way by the police station
and the College Arms toward my own house.
Nothing was burning on the hillside, though
from the common there still came a red glare
and a rolling tumult of ruddy smoke beating

up against the drenching hail. So far as I could
see by the flashes, the houses about me were
mostly uninjured. By the College Arms a dark
heap lay in the road.

Down the road toward Maybury Bridge there
were voices and the sound of feet, but I had not
the courage to shout or to go to them. I let myself in with my latchkey, closed, locked and
bolted the door, staggered to the foot of the
staircase, and sat down. My imagination was
full of those striding metallic monsters, and of
the dead body smashed against the fence.

I crouched at the foot of the staircase with my
back to the wall, shivering violently.

11. At the Window

I HAVE ALREADY SAID that my storms of emotion have a trick of exhausting themselves. After a time I discovered that I was cold and wet, and with little pools of water about me on the stair carpet. I got up almost mechanically, went into the dining room and drank some whiskey, and then I was moved to change my clothes.

After I had done that I went upstairs to my study, but why I did so I do not know. The window of my study looks over the trees and the railway toward Horsell common. In the hurry of our departure this window had been left open. The passage was dark, and, by contrast with the picture the window frame enclosed, the side of the room seemed impenetrably dark. I stopped short in the doorway.

The thunderstorm had passed. The towers of
the Oriental College and the pine trees about it
had gone, and very far away, lit by a vivid red
glare, the common about the sand pits was visible. Across the light, huge black shapes, grotesque and strange, moved busily to and fro.

It seemed indeed as if the whole country in
that direction was on fire — a broad hillside set
with minute tongues of flame, swaying and
writhing with the gusts of the dying storm, and
throwing a red reflection upon the cloud scud
above. Every now and then a haze of smoke
from some nearer conflagration drove across the
window and hid the Martian shapes. I could not
see what they were doing, nor the clear form of
them, nor recognize the black objects they were
busied upon. Neither could I see the nearer fire,
though the reflections of it danced on the wall
and ceiling of the study. A sharp, resinous tang
of burning was in the air.

I closed the door noiselessly and crept toward
the window. As I did so, the view opened out until, on the one hand, it reached to the houses
about Woking station, and on the other to the
charred and blackened pine woods of Byfleet.
There was a light down below the hill, on the
railway, near the arch, and several of the houses
along the Maybury road and the streets near
the station were glowing ruins. The light upon
the railway puzzled me at first; there were a
black heap and a vivid glare, and to the right of

that a row of yellow oblongs. Then I perceived
this was a wrecked train, the forepart smashed
and on fire, the hinder carriages still upon the
rails.

Between these three main centers of light, the
houses, the train, and the burning country toward Chobham, stretched irregular patches of
dark country, broken here and there by intervals of dimly glowing and smoking ground. It
was the strangest spectacle, that black expanse
set with fire. It reminded me, more than anything else, of the potteries at night. At first I
could distinguish no people at all, though I
peered intently for them. Later I saw against
the light of Woking station a number of black
figures hurrying one after the other across the
line.

And this was the little world in which I had
been living securely for years, this fiery chaos!
What had happened in the last seven hours I still
did not know; nor did I know, though I was beginning to guess, the relation between these mechanical colossi and the sluggish lumps I had
seen disgorged from the cylinder. With a queer
feeling of impersonal interest I turned my desk
chair to the window, sat down, and stared at the
blackened country, and particularly at the three
gigantic black things that were going to and fro
in the glare about the sand pits.

They seemed amazingly busy. I began to ask
myself what they could be. Were they intelligent

mechanisms? Such a thing I felt was impossible. Or did a Martian sit within each, ruling, directing, using, much as a man's brain sits and rules in his body? I began to compare the things to human machines, to ask myself for the first time in my life how an ironclad or a steam engine would seem to an intelligent lower animal.

The storm had left the sky clear, and over the smoke of the burning land the little fading pinpoint of Mars was dropping into the west, when a soldier came into my garden. I heard a slight scraping at the fence, and rousing myself from the lethargy that had fallen upon me, I looked down and saw him dimly, clambering over the palings. At the sight of another human being my torpor passed, and I leaned out of the window eagerly.

"Hist!" said I, in a whisper.

He stopped astride of the fence in doubt. Then he came over and across the lawn to the corner of the house. He bent down and stepped softly.

"Who's there?" he said, also whispering, standing under the window and peering up.

"Where are you going?" I asked.

"God knows."

"Are you trying to hide?"

"That's it."

"Come into the house," I said.

I went down, unfastened the door, and let him in, and locked the door again. I could not see his face. He was hatless, and his coat was unbuttoned.

"My God!" he said, as I drew him in.

"What has happened?" I asked.

"What hasn't?" In the obscurity I could see he made a gesture of despair. "They wiped us out — simply wiped us out," he repeated again and again.

He followed me, almost mechanically, into the dining room.

"Take some whiskey," I said, pouring out a stiff dose.

He drank it. Then abruptly he sat down before the table, put his head on his arms, and began to sob and weep like a little boy, in a perfect passion of emotion, while I, with a curious forgetfulness of my own recent despair, stood beside him, wondering.

It was a long time before he could steady his nerves to answer my questions, and then he answered perplexingly and brokenly. He was a driver in the artillery, and had only come into action about seven. At that time firing was going on across the common, and it was said the first party of Martians were crawling slowly toward their second cylinder under cover of a metal shield.

Later this shield staggered up on tripod legs and became the first of the fighting machines I had seen. The gun he drove had been unlimbered near Horsell, in order to command the sand

pits, and its arrival it was that had precipitated
the action. As the limber gunners went to the
rear, his horse trod in a rabbit hole and came
down, throwing him into a depression of the
ground. At the same moment the gun exploded
behind him, the ammunition blew up, there was
fire all about him, and he found himself lying
under a heap of charred dead men and dead
horses.

"I lay still," he said, "scared out of my wits,
with the forequarter of a horse atop of me.
We'd been wiped out. And the smell — good
God! Like burned meat! I was hurt across the
back by the fall of the horse, and there I had to
lie until I felt better. Just like parade it had
been a minute before — then stumble, bang,
swish!

"Wiped out!" he said.

He had hid under the dead horse for a long
time, peeping out furtively across the common.
The Cardigan men had tried a rush, in skirm-
ishing order, at the pit, simply to be swept out
of existence. Then the monster had risen to its
feet, and had begun to walk leisurely to and fro
across the common among the few fugitives,
with its headlike hood turning about exactly
like the head of a cowled human being. A kind
of arm carried a complicated metallic case, about
which green flashes scintillated, and out of the
funnel of this there smote the Heat Ray.

In a few minutes there was, so far as the

soldier could see, not a living thing left upon the
common, and every bush and tree upon it that
was not already a blackened skeleton was burning. The hussars had been on the road beyond
the curvature of the ground, and he saw nothing
of them. He heard the Maxims rattle for a time
and then become still. The giant saved Woking
station and its cluster of houses until the last;
then in a moment the Heat Ray was brought to
bear, and the town became a heap of fiery ruins.
Then the Thing shut off the Heat Ray, and,
turning its back upon the artilleryman, began
to waddle away toward the smoldering pine
woods that sheltered the second cylinder. As it
did so a second glittering Titan built itself up
out of the pit.

The second monster followed the first, and at
that the artilleryman began to crawl very cautiously across the hot heather ash toward Horsell. He managed to get alive into the ditch by
the side of the road, and so escaped to Woking.
There his story became ejaculatory. The place
was impassable. It seems there were a few people alive there, frantic for the most part, and
many burned and scalded. He was turned aside
by the fire, and hid among some almost scorch-
ing heaps of broken wall as one of the Martian
giants returned. He saw this one pursue a man,
catch him up in one of its steely tentacles, and
knock his head against the trunk of a pine tree.
At last, after nightfall, the artilleryman made

a rush for it and got over the railway embankment.

Since then he had been skulking along toward Maybury, in the hope of getting out of danger Londonward. People were hiding in trenches and cellars, and many of the survivors had made off toward Woking village and Send. He had been consumed with thirst until he found one of the water mains near the railway arch smashed, and the water bubbling out like a spring upon the road.

That was the story I got from him, bit by bit. He grew calmer telling me and trying to make me see the things he had seen. He had eaten no food since midday, he told me early in his narrative, and I found some mutton and bread in the pantry and brought it into the room. We lit no lamp for fear of attracting the Martians, and ever and again our hands would touch upon bread or meat. As he talked, things about us came darkly out of the darkness, and the trampled bushes and broken rose trees outside the window grew distinct. It would seem that a number of men or animals had rushed across the lawn. I began to see his face, blackened and haggard, as no doubt mine was also.

When we had finished eating we went softly upstairs to my study, and I looked again out of the open window. In one night the valley had become a valley of ashes. The fires had dwindled now. Where flames had been there were now streamers of smoke; but the countless ruins of shattered and gutted houses and blasted and blackened trees that the night had hidden stood out now gaunt and terrible in the pitiless light of dawn. Yet here and there some object had had the luck to escape — a white railway signal here, the end of a greenhouse there, white and fresh amid the wreçkage. Never before in the history of warfare had destruction been so indiscriminate and so universal. And shining with the growing light of the east, three of the metallic giants stood about the pit, their cowls rotating as though they were surveying the desolation they had made.

It seemed to me that the pit had been enlarged, and ever and again puffs of vivid green vapor streamed up out of it toward the brightening dawn — streamed up, whirled, broke, and vanished.

Beyond were the pillars of fire about Chobham. They became pillars of bloodshot smoke at the first touch of day.

12. What I Saw of the Destruction of Weybridge and Shepperton

As THE DAWN GREW BRIGHTER we withdrew from the window from which we had watched the Martians, and went very quietly downstairs.

The artilleryman agreed with me that the house was no place to stay in. He proposed, he said, to make his way Londonward, and thence rejoin his battery — No. 12, of the Horse Artillery. My plan was to return at once to Leatherhead; and so greatly had the strength of the Martians impressed me that I had determined to take my wife to Newhaven, and go with her out of the country forthwith. For I already perceived clearly that the country about London must inevitably be the scene of a disastrous struggle before such creatures as these could be destroyed.

Between us and Leatherhead, however, lay the Third Cylinder, with its guarding giants. Had I been alone, I think I should have taken my chance and struck across the country. But the artilleryman dissuaded me: "It's no kindness to the right sort of wife," he said, "to make her a widow"; and in the end I agreed to go with him, under cover of the woods, northward as far as Street Cobham before I parted with him. Thence I would make a big detour by Epsom to reach Leatherhead.

I should have started at once, but my companion had been in active service and he knew better than that. He made me ransack the house for a flask, which he filled with whiskey; and we lined every available pocket with packets of biscuits and slices of meat. Then we crept out of the house, and ran as quickly as we could down the ill-made road by which I had come overnight. The houses seemed deserted. In the road lay a group of three charred bodies close together, struck dead by the Heat Ray; and here and there were things that people had dropped — a clock, a slipper, a silver spoon, and the like poor valuables. At the corner turning up toward the post office a little cart, filled with boxes and furniture, and horseless, heeled over on a broken wheel. A cash box had been hastily smashed open and thrown under the débris.

Except the lodge at the orphanage, which was still on fire, none of the houses had suffered very

greatly here. The Heat Ray had shaved the
chimney tops and passed. Yet, save ourselves,
there did not seem to be a living soul on Maybury Hill. The majority of the inhabitants had
escaped, I suppose, by way of the Old Woking
road — the road I had taken when I drove to
Leatherhead — or they had hidden.

We went down the lane, by the body of the
man in black, sodden now from the overnight
hail, and broke into the woods at the foot of the
hill. We pushed through these toward the railway without meeting a soul. The woods across
the line were but the scarred and blackened ruins of woods; for the most part the trees had
fallen, but a certain proportion still stood, dismal gray stems, with dark brown foliage instead
of green.

On our side the fire had done no more than
scorch the nearer trees; it had failed to secure
its footing. In one place the woodmen had been
at work on Saturday; trees, felled and freshly
trimmed, lay in a clearing, with heaps of saw-
dust by the sawing machine and its engine.
Hard by was a temporary hut, deserted. There
was not a breath of wind this morning, and
everything was strangely still. Even the birds
were hushed, and as we hurried along I and the
artilleryman talked in whispers and looked now
and again over our shoulders. Once or twice we
stopped to listen.

After a time we drew near the road, and as

we did so we heard the clatter of hoofs and saw through the tree stems three cavalry soldiers riding slowly toward Woking. We hailed them, and they halted while we hurried toward them. It was a lieutenant and a couple of privates of the 8th Hussars, with a stand like a theodolite, which the artilleryman told me was a heliograph.

"You are the first men I've seen coming this way this morning," said the lieutenant. "What's brewing?"

His voice and face were eager. The men behind him stared curiously. The artilleryman jumped down the bank into the road and saluted.

"Gun destroyed last night, sir. Have been hiding. Trying to rejoin battery, sir. You'll come in sight of the Martians, I expect, about half a mile along this road."

"What the dickens are they like?" asked the lieutenant.

"Giants in armor, sir. Hundred feet high. Three legs and a body like 'luminium, with a mighty great head in a hood, sir."

"Get out!" said the lieutenant. "What confounded nonsense!"

"You'll see, sir. They carry a kind of box, sir, that shoots fire and strikes you dead."

"What d'ye mean — a gun?"

"No, sir," and the artilleryman began a vivid account of the Heat Ray. Halfway through, the lieutenant interrupted him and looked up at me. I was still standing on the bank by the side of the road.

"It's perfectly true," I said.

"Well," said the lieutenant, "I suppose it's my business to see it too. Look here" — to the artilleryman — "we're detailed here clearing people out of their houses. You'd better go along and report yourself to Brigadier General Marvin, and tell him all you know. He's at Weybridge. Know the way?"

"I do," I said; and he turned his horse southward again.

"Half a mile, you say?" said he.

"At most," I answered, and pointed over the treetops southward. He thanked me and rode on, and we saw them no more.

Farther along we came upon a group of three women and two children in the road, busy clearing out a laborer's cottage. They had got hold of a little hand truck, and were piling it up with unclean looking bundles and shabby furniture. They were all too assiduously engaged to talk to us as we passed.

By Byfleet station we emerged from the pine trees, and found the country calm and peaceful under the morning sunlight. We were far beyond the range of the Heat Ray there, and had it not been for the silent desertion of some of the houses, the stirring movement of packing in others, and the knot of soldiers standing on the bridge over the railway and staring down the line toward Woking, the day would have seemed very like any other Sunday.

Several farm wagons and carts were moving creakily along the road to Addlestone, and suddenly through the gate of a field we saw, across a stretch of flat meadow, six twelve-pounders standing neatly at equal distances pointing toward Woking. The gunners stood by the guns waiting, and the ammunition wagons were at a businesslike distance. The men stood almost as if under inspection.

"That's good!" said I. "They will get one fair shot, at any rate."

The artilleryman hesitated at the gate.

"I shall go on," he said.

Farther on toward Weybridge, just over the bridge, there were a number of men in white fatigue jackets throwing up a long rampart, and more guns behind.

"It's bows and arrows against the lightning, anyhow," said the artilleryman. "They 'aven't seen that fire beam yet."

The officers who were not actively engaged stood and stared over the treetops southwestward, and the men digging would stop every now and again to stare in the same direction.

Byfleet was in a tumult; people packing, and a score of hussars, some of them dismounted, some on horseback, were hunting them about. Three or four black government wagons, with crosses in white circles, and an old omnibus, among other vehicles, were being loaded in the village street. There were scores of people, most of them sufficiently sabbatical to have assumed their best clothes. The soldiers were having the greatest difficulty in making them realize the gravity of their position. We saw one shriveled old fellow with a huge box and a score or more of flowerpots containing orchids, angrily expostulating with the corporal who would leave them behind. I stopped and gripped his arm.

"Do you know what's over there?" I said, pointing at the pine tops that hid the Martians.

"Eh?" said he, turning. "I was explainin' these is vallyble."

"Death!" I shouted. "Death is coming! Death!" and leaving him to digest that if he could, I hurried on after the artilleryman. At the corner I looked back. The soldier had left him, and he was still standing by his box, with the pots of orchids on the lid of it, and staring vaguely over the trees.

No one in Weybridge could tell us where the headquarters were established; the whole place was in such confusion as I had never seen in any town before. Carts, carriages everywhere, the most astonishing miscellany of conveyances and horseflesh. The respectable inhabitants of the place, men in golf and boating costumes, wives prettily dressed, were packing, riverside loafers energetically helping, children excited, and, for the most part, highly delighted at this astonishing variation of their Sunday experiences. In the midst of it all the worthy vicar was very pluckily holding an early celebration, and his bell was jangling out above the excitement.

I and the artilleryman, seated on the step of the drinking fountain, made a very passable meal upon what we had brought with us. Patrols of soldiers — here no longer hussars, but grenadiers in white — were warning people to move now or to take refuge in their cellars as soon as the firing began. We saw as we crossed the railway bridge that a growing crowd of people had assembled in and about the railway station, and the swarming platform was piled with boxes and packages. The ordinary traffic had been stopped, I believe, in order to allow of the passage of troops and guns to Chertsey, and I have heard since that a savage struggle occurred for places in the special trains that were put on at a later hour.

We remained at Weybridge until midday, and at that hour we found ourselves at the place near Shepperton Lock where the Wey and Thames join. Part of the time we spent helping two old women to pack a little cart. The Wey has a treble mouth, and at this point boats are to be hired, and there was a ferry across the river. On the Shepperton side was an inn with a lawn, and beyond that the tower

of Shepperton Church — it has been replaced
by a spire — rose above the trees.

Here we found an excited and noisy crowd
of fugitives. As yet the flight had not grown
to a panic, but there were already far more
people than all the boats going to and fro
could enable to cross. People came panting along
under heavy burdens; one husband and wife
were even carrying a small outhouse door between them, with some of their household goods
piled thereon. One man told us he meant to
try to get away from Shepperton station.

There was a lot of shouting, and one man
was even jesting. The idea people seemed to
have here was that the Martians were simply
formidable human beings, who might attack
and sack the town, to be certainly destroyed in
the end. Every now and then people would
glance nervously across the Wey, at the meadows toward Chertsey, but everything over
there was still.

Across the Thames, except just where the
boats landed, everything was quiet, in vivid
contrast with the Surrey side. The people who
landed there from the boats went tramping off
down the lane. The big ferry boat had just
made a journey. Three or four soldiers stood
on the lawn of the inn, staring and jesting at
the fugitives, without offering to help. The inn
was closed, as it was now within prohibited
hours.

"What's that?" cried a boatman, and "Shut up, you fool!" said a man near me to a yelping dog. Then the sound came again, this time from the direction of Chertsey, a muffled thud — the sound of a gun.

The fighting was beginning. Almost immediately unseen batteries across the river to our right, unseen because of the trees, took up the chorus, firing heavily one after the other. A woman screamed. Everyone stood arrested by the sudden stir of battle, near us and yet invisible to us. Nothing was to be seen save flat meadows, cows feeding unconcernedly for the most part, and silvery pollard willows motionless in the warm sunlight.

"The sojers'll stop 'em," said a woman beside me, doubtfully. A haziness rose over the tree-tops.

Then suddenly we saw a rush of smoke far away up the river, a puff of smoke that jerked up into the air and hung; and forthwith the ground heaved underfoot and a heavy explosion shook the air, smashing two or three windows in the houses near, and leaving us astonished.

"Here they are!" shouted a man in a blue jersey. "Yonder! D'yer see them? Yonder!"

Quickly, one after the other, one, two, three, four of the armored Martians appeared, far away over the little trees, across the flat meadows that stretched toward Chertsey, and

striding hurriedly toward the river. Little
cowled figures they seemed at first, going with
a rolling motion and as fast as flying birds.

Then, advancing obliquely toward us, came
a fifth. Their armored bodies glittered in the
sun as they swept swiftly forward upon the
guns, growing rapidly larger as they drew
nearer. One on the extreme left, the remotest
that is, flourished a huge case high in the air,
and the ghostly, terrible Heat Ray I had already seen on Friday night smote toward
Chertsey, and struck the town.

At sight of these strange, swift, and terrible
creatures the crowd near the water's edge seemed
to me to be for a moment horror-struck. There
was no screaming or shouting, but a silence.
Then a hoarse murmur and a movement of
feet — a splashing from the water. A man,
too frightened to drop the portmanteau he
carried on his shoulder, swung round and sent
me staggering with a blow from the corner of
his burden. A woman thrust at me with her
hand and rushed past me. I turned with the
rush of the people, but I was not too terrified
for thought. The terrible Heat Ray was in my
mind. To get under water! That was it!

"Get under water!" I shouted, unheeded.

I faced about again, and rushed toward the
approaching Martian, rushed right down the
gravelly beach and headlong into the water.
Others did the same. A boatload of people put-

ting back came leaping out as I rushed past.
The stones under my feet were muddy and
slippery, and the river was so low that I ran
perhaps twenty feet scarcely waist-deep. Then,
as the Martian towered overhead scarcely a
couple of hundred yards away, I flung myself
forward under the surface. The splashes of the
people in the boats leaping into the river
sounded like thunderclaps in my ears. People
were landing hastily on both sides of the river.

But the Martian machine took no more notice for the moment of the people running
this way and that than a man would of the
confusion of ants in a nest against which his
foot has kicked. When, half-suffocated, I raised
my head above water, the Martian's hood
pointed at the batteries that were still firing
across the river, and as it advanced, it swung
loose what must have been the generator of
the Heat Ray.

In another moment it was on the bank, and
in a stride wading halfway across. The knees
of its foremost legs bent at a farther bank,
and in another moment it had raised itself to
its full height again, close to the village of
Shepperton. Forthwith the six guns which, unknown to anyone on the right bank, had been
hidden behind the outskirts of that village,
fired simultaneously. The sudden near concussion, the last close upon the first, made my
heart jump. The monster was already raising

the case generating the Heat Ray as the first
shell burst six yards above the hood.

I gave a cry of astonishment. I saw and
thought nothing of the other four Martian
monsters; my attention was riveted upon the
nearer incident. Simultaneously two other
shells burst in the air near the body as the
hood twisted round in time to receive, but not
in time to dodge, the fourth shell.

The shell burst clean in the face of the Thing.
The hood bulged, flashed, was whirled off in a
dozen tattered fragments of red flesh and glittering metal.

"Hit!" shouted I, with something between
a scream and a cheer.

I heard answering shouts from the people
in the water about me. I could have leaped out
of the water with that momentary exultation.

The decapitated colossus reeled like a drunken
giant; but it did not fall over. It recovered its
balance by a miracle, and, no longer heeding
its steps and with the camera that fired the
Heat Ray now rigidly upheld, it reeled swiftly
upon Shepperton. The living intelligence, the
Martian within the hood, was slain and
splashed to the four winds of heaven, and the
Thing was now but a mere intricate device of
metal whirling to destruction. It drove along in
a straight line, incapable of guidance. It struck
the tower of Shepperton Church, smashing it
down as the impact of a battering ram might

have done, swerved aside, blundered on, and collapsed with tremendous force into the river out of my sight.

A violent explosion shook the air, and a spout of water, steam, mud, and shattered metal shot far up into the sky. As the camera of the Heat Ray hit the water, the latter had immediately flashed into steam. In another moment a huge wave, like a muddy tidal bore but almost scaldingly hot, came sweeping round the bend upstream. I saw people struggling shoreward, and heard their screaming and shouting faintly above the seething and roar of the Martian's collapse.

For a moment I heeded nothing of the heat, forgot the patent need of self-preservation. I splashed through the tumultuous water, pushing aside a man in black to do so, until I could see round the bend. Half a dozen deserted boats pitched aimlessly upon the confusion of the waves. The fallen Martian came into sight downstream, lying across the river, and for the most part submerged.

Thick clouds of steam were pouring off the wreckage, and through the tumultuously whirling wisps I could see, intermittently and vaguely, the gigantic limbs churning the water and flinging a splash and spray of mud and froth into the air. The tentacles swayed and struck like living arms, and, save for the helpless purposelessness of these movements, it was as

if some wounded thing were struggling for its
life amid the waves. Enormous quantities of a
ruddy-brown fluid were spurting up in noisy
jets out of the machine.

My attention was diverted from this death
flurry by a furious yelling, like that of the
thing called a siren in our manufacturing
towns. A man, knee-deep near the towing path,
shouted inaudibly to me and pointed. Looking
back, I saw the other Martians advancing with
gigantic strides down the riverbank from the
direction of Chertsey. The Shepperton guns
spoke this time unavailingly.

At that I ducked at once under water, and,
holding my breath until movement was an
agony, blundered painfully ahead under the
surface as long as I could. The water was in a
tumult about me, and rapidly growing hotter.

When for a moment I raised my head to
take breath and throw the hair and water
from my eyes, the steam was rising in a whirling white fog that at first hid the Martians
altogether. The noise was deafening. Then I
saw them dimly, colossal figures of gray, magni-
fied by the mist. They had passed by me, and
two were stooping over the frothing, tumultuous ruins of their comrade.

The third and fourth stood beside him in
the water, one perhaps two hundred yards from
me, the other toward Laleham. The genera-
tors of the Heat Rays waved high, and the

hissing beams smote down this way and that.

The air was full of sound, a deafening and confusing conflict of noises — the clangorous din of Martians, the crash of falling houses, the thud of trees, fences, sheds flashing into flame, and the crackling and roaring of fire. Dense black smoke was leaping up to mingle with the steam from the river, and as the Heat Ray went to and fro over Weybridge its impact was marked by flashes of incandescent white that gave place at once to a smoky dance of lurid flames. The nearer houses still stood intact, awaiting their fate, shadowy faint, and pallid in the steam, with the fire behind them going to and fro.

For a moment perhaps I stood there, breast-high in the almost boiling water, dumbfounded at my position, hopeless of escape. Through the reek I could see the people who had been with me in the river scrambling out of the water through the reeds, like little frogs hurrying through grass from the advance of a man, or running to and fro in utter dismay on the towing path.

Then suddenly the white flashes of the Heat Ray came leaping toward me. The houses caved in as they dissolved at its touch, and darted out flames; the trees changed to fire with a roar. The Ray flickered up and down the towing path, licking off the people who ran this way and that, and came down to the water's edge not fifty yards from where I stood. It swept across the river to Shepperton, and the water in its track rose in a boiling weal crested with stream. I turned shoreward.

In another moment the huge wave, well nigh at the boiling point, had rushed upon me. I screamed aloud, and scalded, half blinded, agonized, I staggered through the leaping, hissing water toward the shore. Had my foot stumbled, it would have been the end. I fell helplessly, in full sight of the Martians, upon the broad, bare gravelly spit that runs down to mark the angle of the Wey and Thames. I expected nothing but death.

I have a dim memory of the foot of a Martian coming down within a score of yards of my head, driving straight into the loose gravel, whirling it this way and that, and lifting again; of a long suspense, and then of the four carrying the débris of their comrade between them, now clear and then presently faint through a veil of smoke, receding interminably, as it seemed to me, across a vast space of river and meadow. And then, very slowly, I realized that by a miracle I had escaped.

13. How I Fell in with the Curate

AFTER GETTING THIS SUDDEN LESSON in the power of terrestrial weapons, the Martians retreated to their original position upon Horsell Common; and in their haste, and encumbered with the débris of their smashed companion, they no doubt overlooked many such a stray and negligible victim as myself. Had they left their comrade and pushed on forthwith, there was nothing at that time between them and London but batteries of twelve-pounder guns, and they would certainly have reached the capital in advance of the tidings of their approach; as sudden, dreadful, and destructive their advent would have been as the earthquake that destroyed Lisbon a century ago.

But they were in no hurry. Cylinder followed

cylinder on its interplanetary flight; every
twenty-four hours brought them reinforce-
ment. And meanwhile the military and naval
authorities, now fully alive to the tremendous
power of their antagonists, worked with furious energy. Every minute a fresh gun came
into position until, before twilight, every copse,
every row of suburban villas on the hilly slopes
about Kingston and Richmond, masked an expectant black muzzle. And through the charred
and desolated area — perhaps twenty square
miles altogether — that encircled the Martian
encampment on Horsell Ccmmon, through
charred and ruined villages among the green
trees, through the blackened and smoking
arcades that had been but a day ago pine spin-
neys, crawled the devoted scouts with the heliographs that were presently to warn the gunners
of the Martian approach. But the Martians now
understood our command of artillery and the
danger of human proximity, and not a man ventured within a mile of either cylinder, save at the
price of his life.

It would seem that these giants spent the
earlier part of the afternoon in going to and
fro, transferring everything from the second
and third cylinders — the second in Addlestone
Golf Links and the third at Pyrford — to their
original pit on Horsell Common. Over that,
above the blackened heather and ruined buildings that stretched far and wide, stood one as

sentinel, while the rest abandoned their vast fighting machines and descended into the pit. They were hard at work there far into the night, and the towering pillar of dense green smoke that rose therefrom could be seen from the hills about Merrow, and even, it is said, from Banstead and Epsom Downs.

And while the Martians behind me were thus preparing for their next sally, and in front of me humanity gathered for the battle, I made my way with infinite pains and labor from the fire and smoke of burning Weybridge toward London.

I saw an abandoned boat, very small and remote, drifting downstream; and throwing off most of my sodden clothes, I went after it, gained it, and so escaped out of that destruction. There were no oars in the boat, but I contrived to paddle, as well as my parboiled hands would allow, down the river toward Halliford and Walton, going very tediously and continually looking behind me, as you may well understand. I followed the river, because I considered that the water gave me my best chance of escape should these giants return.

The hot water from the Martian's overthrow drifted downstream with me, so that for the best part of a mile I could see little of either bank. Once, however, I made out a string of black figures hurrying across the meadows from the direction of Weybridge. Halliford, it

seemed, was deserted, and several of the houses
facing the river were on fire. It was strange to
see the place quite tranquil, quite desolate under
the hot, blue sky, with the smoke and little
threads of flame going straight up into the
heat of the afternoon. Never before had I seen
houses burning without the accompaniment of
an obstructive crowd. A little farther on the
dry reeds up the bank were smoking and glowing, and a line of fire inland was marching
steadily across a late field of hay.

For a long time I drifted, so painful and
weary was I after the violence I had been
through, and so intense the heat upon the water. Then my fears got the better of me again,
and I resumed my paddling. The sun scorched
my bare back. At last, as the bridge at Walton
was coming into sight round the bend, my
fever and faintness overcame my fears, and I
landed on the Middlesex bank and lay down,
deadly sick, amid the long grass. I suppose the
time was then about four or five o'clock. I got
up presently, walked perhaps half a mile without meeting a soul, and then lay down again
in the shadow of a hedge. I seem to remember
talking, wanderingly, to myself during that last
spurt. I was also very thirsty, and bitterly re-
gretful I had drunk no more water. It is a
curious thing that I felt angry with my wife;
I cannot account for it, but my impotent desire
to reach Leatherhead worried me excessively.

I do not clearly remember the arrival of the curate, so that probably I dozed. I became aware of him as a seated figure in soot-smudged shirtsleeves, and with his upturned clean-shaven face staring at a faint flickering that danced over the sky. The sky was what is called a mackeral sky — rows and rows of faint downplumes of cloud, just tinted with the mid-summer sunset.

I sat up, and at the rustle of my motion he looked at me quickly.

"Have you any water?" I asked abruptly.

He shook his head.

"You have been asking for water for the last hour," he said.

For a moment we were silent, taking stock of each other. I dare say he found me a strange enough figure, naked, save for my water-soaked trousers and socks, scalded, and my face and shoulders blackened by the smoke. His face was a fair weakness, his chin retreated, and his hair lay in crisp, almost flaxen curls on his low forehead; his eyes were rather large, pale blue, and blankly staring. He spoke abruptly, looking vacantly away from me.

"What does it mean?" he said. "What do these things mean?"

I stared at him and made no answer.

He extended a thin white hand and spoke in almost a complaining tone.

"Why are these things permitted? What sins

have we done? The morning service was over,
I was walking through the roads to clear my
brain for the afternoon, and then — fire,
earthquake, death! As if it were Sodom and
Gomorrah! All our work undone, all the work
— What are these Martians?"

"What are we?" I answered, clearing my
throat.

He gripped his knees and turned to look at
me again. For half a minute, perhaps, he stared
silently.

"I was walking through the roads to clear
my brain," he said. "And suddenly — fire,
earthquake, death!"

He relapsed into silence, with his chin now
sunken almost to his knees.

Presently he began waving his hand.

"All the work — all the Sunday-schools —
What have we done — what has Weybridge
done? Everything gone — everything destroyed. The church! We rebuilt it only three
years ago. Gone! — swept out of existence!
Why?"

Another pause, and he broke out again like one
demented.

"The smoke of her burning goeth up for ever
and ever!" he shouted.

His eyes flamed, and he pointed a lean finger
in the direction of Weybridge.

By this time I was beginning to take his
measure. The tremendous tragedy in which he

had been involved — it was evident he was a
fugitive from Weybridge — had driven him to
the very verge of his reason.

"Are we far from Sunbury?" I said, in a
matter-of-fact tone.

"What are we to do?" he asked. "Are these
creatures everywhere? Has the earth been given
over to them?"

"Are we far from Sunbury?"

"Only this morning I officiated at early celebration ——"

"Things have changed," I said, quietly. "You
must keep your head. There is still hope."

"Hope!"

"Yes. Plentiful hope — for all this destruction!"

I began to explain my view of our position.
He listened at first, but as I went on the interest dawning in his eyes gave place to their former stare, and his regard wandered from me.

"This must be the beginning of the end,"
he said, interrupting me. "The end! The great
and terrible day of the Lord! When men shall
call upon the mountains and the rocks to fall
upon them and hide them — hide them from
the face of Him that sitteth upon the throne!"

I began to understand the position. I ceased
my labored reasoning, struggled to my feet,
and, standing over him, laid my hand on his
shoulder.

"Be a man!" said I. "You are scared out of

your wits! What good is religion if it collapses
under calamity? Think of what earthquakes
and floods, wars and volcanoes, have done before to men! Did you think God had exempted
Weybridge? He is not an insurance agent."

For a time he sat in blank silence.

"But how can we escape?" he asked, suddenly."
"They are invulnerable, they are pitiless."

"Neither the one, nor, perhaps, the other,"
I answered. "And the mightier they are the
more sane and wary should we be. One of them
was killed yonder not three hours ago."

"Killed!" he said, staring about him. "How
can God's ministers be killed?"

"I saw it happen." I proceeded to tell him.
"We have chanced to come in for the thick of
it," said I, "and that is all."

"What is that flicker in the sky?" he asked
abruptly.

I told him it was the heliograph signaling —
that it was the sign of human help and effort
in the sky.

"We are in the midst of it," I said, "quiet as it
is. That flicker in the sky tells of the gathering
storm. Yonder, I take it, are the Martians, and
Londonward, where those hills rise about
Richmond and Kingston and the trees give
cover, earthworks are being thrown up and guns
are being placed. Presently the Martians will
be coming this way again."

And even as I spoke he sprang to his feet and stopped me by a gesture.

"Listen!" he said.

From beyond the low hills across the water came the dull resonance of distant guns and a remote weird crying. Then everything was still. A cockchafer came droning over the hedge and past us. High in the west the crescent moon hung faint and pale above the smoke of Weybridge and Shepperton and the hot, still splendor of the sunset.

"We had better follow this path," I said, "northward."

14. In London

My younger brother was in London when the Martians fell at Woking. He was a medical student, working for an imminent examination, and he heard nothing of the arrival until Saturday morning. The morning papers on Saturday contained, in addition to lengthy special articles on the planet Mars, on life in the planets, and so forth, a brief and vaguely worded telegram, all the more striking for its brevity.

The Martians, alarmed by the approach of a crowd, had killed a number of people with a quick-firing gun, so the story ran. The telegram concluded with the words: "Formidable as they seem to be, the Martians have not moved from the pit into which they have fallen, and, indeed, seem incapable of doing so. Prob-

ably this is due to the relative strength of the
earth's gravitational energy." On that last
text their leader writer expanded very com-
fortingly.

Of course all the students in the crammer's biology class, to which my brother went that day,
were intensely interested, but there were no
signs of any unusual excitement in the streets.
The afternoon papers puffed scraps of news
under big headlines. They had nothing to tell
beyond the movements of troops about the
common, and the burning of the pine woods
between Woking and Weybridge, until eight.
Then, the *St. James's Gazette,* in an extra special edition, announced the bare fact of the
interruption of telegraphic communication. This
was thought to be due to the falling of burning
pine trees across the line. Nothing more of the
fighting was known that night, the night of
my drive to Leatherhead and back.

My brother felt no anxiety about us, as he
knew from the description in the papers that
the cylinder was a good two miles from my
house. He made up his mind to run down that
night to me, in order, as he says, to see the
Things before they were killed. He dispatched
a telegram, which never reached me, about four
o'clock, and spent the evening at a music hall.

In London, also, on Saturday night there was
a thunderstorm, and my brother reached Waterloo in a cab. On the platform from which the

midnight train usually starts he learned, after
some waiting, that an accident prevented trains
from reaching Woking that night. The nature
of the accident he could not ascertain; indeed,
the railway authorities did not clearly know at
that time. There was very little excitement in
the station, as the officials, failing to realize
that anything further than a breakdown between Byfleet and Woking junction had occurred, were running the theatre trains which
usually passed through Woking, round by Vir-
ginia Water or Guildford. They were busy
making the necessary arrangements to alter the
route of the Southampton and Portsmouth
Sunday League excursions. A nocturnal newspaper reporter, mistaking my brother for the
traffic manager, to whom he bears a slight resemblance, waylaid and tried to interview him.
Few people, excepting the railway officials, connected the breakdown with the Martians.

I have read, in another account of these events,
that on Sunday morning "all London was
electrified by the news from Woking." As a
matter of fact, there was nothing to justify
that very extravagant phrase. Plenty of Londoners did not hear of the Martians until the
panic of Monday morning. Those who did took
some time to realize all that the hastily worded
telegrams in the Sunday papers conveyed. The
majority of people in London do not read Sunday papers.

The habit of personal security, moreover, is
so deeply fixed in the Londoner's mind, and
startling intelligence so much a matter of
course in the papers, that they could read without any personal tremors: "About seven o'clock
last night the Martians came out of the cylinder, and, moving about under an armor of
metallic shields, have completely wrecked Woking station with the adjacent houses, and
massacred an entire battalion of the Cardigan
Regiment. No details are known. Maxims have
been absolutely useless against their armor;
the field guns have been disabled by them.
Flying hussars have been galloping to Chertsey. The Martians appear to be moving slowly
toward Chertsey or Windsor. Great anxiety
prevails in West Surrey, and earthworks are
being thrown up to check the advance Londonward." That was how the Sunday *Sun* put it,
and a clever and remarkably prompt "hand-
book" article in the *Referee* compared the affair
to a menagerie suddenly let loose in a village.

No one in London knew positively of the
nature of the armored Martians, and there was
still a fixed idea that these monsters must
be sluggish: "crawling," "creeping painfully"
—such expressions occurred in almost all the
earlier reports. None of the telegrams could
have been written by an eyewitness of their
advance. The Sunday papers printed separate
editions as further news came to hand, some

even in default of it. But there was practically
nothing more to tell people until late in the
afternoon, when the authorities gave the press
agencies the news in their possession. It was
stated that the people of Walton and Weybridge, and all the district, were pouring along
the roads Londonward, and that was all.

My brother went to church at the Foundling
Hospital in the morning, still in ignorance of
what had happened on the previous night.
There he heard allusions made to the invasion,
and a special prayer for peace. Coming out, he
bought a *Referee*. He became alarmed at the
news in this, and went again to Waterloo
station to find out if communication were restored. The omnibuses, carriages, cyclists, and
innumerable people walking in their best
clothes seemed scarcely affected by the strange
intelligence that the news venders were dis-
seminating. People were interested, or, if
alarmed, alarmed only on account of the local
residents. At the station he heard for the first
time that the Windsor and Chertsey lines were
now interrupted. The porters told him that
several remarkable telegrams had been received in the morning from Byfleet and Chertsey stations, but that these had abruptly
ceased. My brother could get very little precise
detail out of them. "There's fighting going on
about Weybridge" was the extent of their information.

The train service was now very much disorganized. Quite a number of people who had been expecting friends from places on the Southwestern network were standing about the station. One gray-headed old gentleman came and abused the Southwestern Company bitterly to my brother. "It wants showing up," he said.

One or two trains came in from Richmond, Putney, and Kingston, containing people who had gone out for a day's boating and found the locks closed and a feeling of panic in the air. A man in a blue-and-white blazer addressed my brother, full of strange tidings.

"There's hosts of people driving into Kingston in traps and carts and things, with boxes of valuables and all that," he said. "They come from Molesey and Weybridge and Walton, and they say there's been guns heard at Chertsey, heavy firing, and that mounted soldiers have told them to get off at once because the Martians are coming. *We* heard guns firing at Hampton Court station, but we thought it was thunder. What the dickens does it all mean? The Martians can't get out of their pit, can they?"

My brother could not tell him.

Afterward he found that the vague feeling of alarm had spread to the clients of the underground railway, and that the Sunday excursionists began to return from all over the

Southwestern "lung" — Barnes, Wimbledon,
Richmond Park, Kew, and so forth — at unnaturally early hours; but not a soul had anything more than vague hearsay to tell of. Everyone connected with the terminus seemed ill-
tempered.

About five o'clock the gathering crowd in the
station was immensely excited by the opening
of the line of communication, which is almost
invariably closed, between the Southeastern
and the Southwestern stations, and the passage of carriage trucks bearing huge guns and
carriages crammed with soldiers. These were
the guns that were brought up from Woolwich
and Chatham to cover Kingston. There was
an exchange of pleasantries: "You'll get
eaten!" "We're the beast-tamers!" and so
forth. A little while after that a squad of police
came into the station and began to clear the
public off the platforms, and my brother went
out into the street again.

The church bells were ringing for evensong,
and a squad of Salvation Army lassies came
singing down Waterloo Road. On the bridge a
number of loafers were watching a curious
brown scum that came drifting down the stream
in patches. The sun was just setting, and the
Clock Tower and the Houses of Parliament
rose against one of the most peaceful skies it
is possible to imagine, a sky of gold, barred
with long transverse stripes of reddish-purple

cloud. There was talk of a floating body. One of the men there, a reservist he said he was, told my brother he had seen the heliograph flickering in the west.

In Wellington Street my brother met a couple of sturdy roughs who had just rushed out of Fleet Street with still wet newspapers and staring placards. "Dreadful catastrophe!" they bawled one to the other down Wellington Street. "Fighting at Weybridge! Full Description! Repulse of the Martians! London in Danger!" He had to give threepence for a copy of that paper.

Then it was, and then only, that he realized something of the full power and terror of these monsters. He learned that they were not merely a handful of small sluggish creatures, but that they were minds swaying vast mechanical bodies; and that they could move swiftly and smite with such power that even the mightiest guns could not stand against them.

They were described as "vast spiderlike machines, nearly a hundred feet high, capable of the speed of an express train, and able to shoot out a beam of intense heat." Masked batteries, chiefly of field guns, had been planted in the country about Horsell Common, and especially between the Woking district and London. Five of the machines had been seen moving toward the Thames, and one, by a happy chance, had been destroyed. In the other cases the shells had missed, and the batteries had been at once

annihilated by the Heat Rays. Heavy losses of
soldiers were mentioned, but the tone of the
dispatch was optimistic.

The Martians had been repulsed; they were
not invulnerable. They had retreated to their
triangle of cylinders again, in the circle about
Woking. Signalers with heliographs were
pushing forward upon them from all sides.
Guns were in rapid transit from Windsor,
Portsmouth, Aldershot, Woolwich — even from
the north; among others, long wire guns of
ninety-five tons from Woolwich. Altogether
one hundred and sixteen were in position or
being hastily placed, chiefly covering London.
Never before in England had there been such
a vast or rapid concentration of military material.

Any further cylinders that fell, it was
hoped, could be destroyed at once by high explosives, which were being rapidly manufac-
tured and distributed. No doubt, ran the report,
the situation was of the strangest and gravest
description, but the public was exhorted to
avoid and discourage panic. No doubt the Martians were strange and terrible in the extreme,
but at the outside there could not be more than
twenty of them against our millions.

The authorities had reason to suppose, from
the size of the cylinders, that at the outside
there could not be more than five in each cylinder — fifteen altogether. And one at least was

disposed of — perhaps more. The public would
be fairly warned of the approach of danger,
and elaborate measures were being taken for
the protection of the people in the threatened
southwestern suburbs. And so, with reiterated
assurances of the safety of London and the
ability of the authorities to cope with the difficulty, this quasi-proclamation closed.

This was printed in enormous type on paper so fresh that it was still wet, and there had
been no time to add a word of comment. It was
curious, my brother said, to see how ruthlessly
the usual contents of the paper had been
hacked and taken out to give this place.

All down Wellington Street people could
be seen fluttering out the pink sheets and reading, and the Strand was suddenly noisy with
the voices of an army of hawkers following
these pioneers. Men came scrambling off buses
to secure copies. Certainly this news excited people intensely, whatever their previous apathy.
The shutters of a map-shop in the Strand were
being taken down, my brother said, and a man
in his Sunday raiment, lemon-yellow gloves,
even, was visible inside the window hastily fast-
ening maps of Surrey to the glass.

Going on along the Strand to Trafalgar
Square, the paper in his hand, my brother saw
some of the fugitives from West Surrey. There
was a man with his wife and two boys and some
articles of furniture in a cart such as green

grocers use. He was driving from the direction
of Westminster Bridge; and close behind him
came a hay wagon with five or six respectable-
looking people in it, and some boxes and bundles. The faces of these people were haggard,
and their entire appearance contrasted conspic-
uously with the Sabbath-best appearance of
the people on the omnibuses. People in fashion-
able clothing peeped at them out of cabs. They
stopped at the Square as if undecided which
way to take, and finally turned eastward along
the Strand. Some way behind these came a
man in work-day clothes, riding one of those
old-fashioned tricycles with a small front-
wheel. He was dirty and white in the face.

My brother turned down toward Victoria,
and met a number of such people. He had a
vague idea that he might see something of me.
He noticed an unusual number of police regu-
lating the traffic. Some of the refugees were
exchanging news with the people on the omnibuses. One was professing to have seen the
Martians. "Boilers on stilts, I tell you, striding
along like men." Most of them were excited
and animated by their strange experience.

Beyond Victoria the public houses were doing
a lively trade with these arrivals. At all the
street corners groups of people were reading
papers, talking excitedly, or staring at these
unusual Sunday visitors. They seemed to increase as night drew on, until at last the roads,

my brother said, were like Epsom High Street on a Derby Day. My brother addressed several of these fugitives and got unsatisfactory answers from most.

None of them could tell him any news of Woking except one man, who assured him that Woking had been entirely destroyed on the previous night.

"I come from Byfleet," he said; "a man on a bicycle came through the place in the early morning, and ran from door to door warning us to come away. Then came soldiers. We went out to look, and there were clouds of smoke to the south — nothing but smoke, and not a soul coming that way. Then we heard the guns at Chertsey, and folks coming from Weybridge. So I've locked up my house and come on."

At that time there was a strong feeling in the streets that the authorities were to blame for their incapacity to dispose of the invaders without all this inconvenience.

About eight o'clock a noise of heavy firing was distinctly audible all over the south of London. My brother could not hear it for the traffic in the main thoroughfares, but by striking through the quiet back streets to the river he was able to distinguish it quite plainly.

He walked from Westminster to his apartment near Regent's Park, about two. He was now very anxious on my account, and disturbed at the evident magnitude of the trouble. His

mind was inclined to run, even as mine had
run on Saturday, on military details. He
thought of all those silent, expectant guns, of
the suddenly nomadic countryside; he tried to
imagine "boilers on stilts" a hundred feet high.

There were one or two cart loads of refugees
passing along Oxford Street, and several in
the Marylebone Road, but so slowly was the
news spreading that Regent Street and Port-
land Place were full of their usual Sunday-
night promenaders, albeit they talked in
groups, and along the edge of Regent's Park
there were as many silent couples "walking
out" together under the scattered gas lamps as
ever there had been. The night was warm and
still, and a little oppressive; the sound of guns
continued intermittently, and after midnight
there seemed to be sheet-lightning in the south.

He read and reread the paper, fearing the
worst had happened to me. He was restless, and
after supper prowled out again aimlessly. He
returned and tried in vain to divert his attention to his examination notes. He went to bed
a little after midnight, and was awakened from
lurid dreams in the small hours of Monday
by the sound of door knockers, feet running in
the street, distant drumming, and a clamor of
bells. Red reflections danced on the ceiling. For
a moment he lay astonished, wondering whether
day had come or the world gone mad. Then he
jumped out of bed and ran to the window.

His room was an attic and as he thrust his
head out, up and down the street there were a
dozen echoes to the noise of his window sash,
and heads in every kind of night disarray appeared. Inquiries were being shouted. "They
are coming!" bawled a policeman, hammering
at the door; "the Martians are coming!" and
hurried to the next door.

The sound of drumming and trumpeting
came from the Albany Street Barracks, and
every church within earshot was hard at work
killing sleep with a vehement disorderly toc-
sin. There was a noise of doors opening, and
window after window in the houses opposite
flashed from darkness into yellow illumination.

Up the street came galloping a closed carriage,
bursting abruptly into noise at the corner, rising to a clattering climax under the window,
and dying away slowly in the distance. Close
on the rear of this came a couple of cabs, the
forerunners of a long procession of flying vehicles, going for the most part to Chalk Farm
station, where the Northwestern special trains
were loading up, instead of coming down the
gradient into Euston.

For a long time my brother stared out of
the window in blank astonishment, watching
the policemen hammering at door after door,
and delivering their incomprehensible message.
Then the door behind him opened, and a man
who lodged across the landing came in, dressed

only in shirt, trousers, and slippers, his braces loose about his waist, his hair disordered from his pillow.

"What the devil is it?" he asked. "A fire? What a devil of a row!"

They both craned their heads out of the window, straining to hear what the policemen were shouting. People were coming out of the side streets, and standing in groups at the corners talking.

"What the devil is it all about?" said my brother's fellow-lodger.

My brother answered him vaguely and began to dress, running with each garment to the window in order to miss nothing of the growing excitement. And presently men selling unnaturally early newspapers came bawling into the street:

"London in danger of suffocation! The Kingston and Richmond defenses forced! Fearful massacres in the Thames Valley!"

And all about him — in the rooms below, in the houses on each side and across the road, and behind in the Park Terraces and in the hundred other streets of that part of Marylebone, and the Westbourne Park district and St. Pancras, and westward and northward in Kilburn and St. John's Wood and Hampstead, and eastward in Shoreditch and Highbury and Haggerston and Hoxton, and, indeed, through all the vastness of London from Ealing to

East Ham — people were rubbing their eyes, and opening windows to stare out and ask aimless questions, and dressing hastily as the first breath of the coming storm of Fear blew through the streets. It was the dawn of the great panic. London, which had gone to bed on Sunday night oblivious and inert, was awakened, in the small hours of Monday morning to a vivid sense of danger.

Unable from his window to learn what was happening, my brother went down and out into the street, just as the sky between the parapets of the houses grew pink with the early dawn. The flying people on foot and in vehicles grew more numerous every moment. "Black Smoke!" he heard people crying, and again "Black Smoke!" The contagion of such a unanimous fear was inevitable. As my brother hesitated on the doorstep, he saw another news vender approaching, and got a paper forthwith. The man was running away with the rest, and selling his papers for a shilling each as he ran — a grotesque mingling of profit and panic.

And from this paper my brother read that catastrophic despatch of the Commander in Chief:

"The Martians are able to discharge enormous clouds of a black and poisonous vapor by means of rockets. They have smothered our batteries, destroyed Richmond, Kingston, and

Wimbledon, and are advancing slowly toward London, destroying everything on the way. It is impossible to stop them. There is no safety from the Black Smoke but in instant flight."

That was all, but it was enough. The whole population of the great six-million city was stirring, slipping, running; presently it would be pouring *en masse* northward.

"Black Smoke!" the voices cried. "Fire!"

The bells of the neighboring church made a jangling tumult, a cart carelessly driven smashed, amid shrieks and curses, against the water trough up the street. Sickly yellow lights went to and fro in the houses, and some of the passing cabs flaunted unextinguished lamps. And overhead the dawn was growing brighter, clear and steady and calm.

He heard footsteps running to and fro in the rooms, and up and down stairs behind him. His landlady came to the door, loosely wrapped in dressing gown and shawl; her husband followed ejaculating.

As my brother began to realize the import of all these things, he turned hastily to his own room, put all his available money — some ten pounds altogether — into his pockets, and went out again into the streets.

15. What Had Happened in Surrey

IT WAS while the curate had sat and talked so wildly to me under the hedge in the flat meadows near Halliford, and while my brother was watching the fugitives stream over Westminster Bridge, that the Martians had resumed the offensive. So far as one can ascertain from the conflicting accounts that have been put forth, the majority of them remained busied with preparations in the Horsell pit until nine that night, hurrying on some operation that disengaged huge volumes of green smoke.

But three certainly came out about eight o'clock, and, advancing slowly and cautiously, made their way through Byfleet and Pyrford toward Ripley and Weybridge, and so came in sight of the expectant batteries against the

setting sun. These Martians did not advance in
body, but in a line, each perhaps a mile and a
half from his nearest fellow. They communicated with one another by means of siren like
howls, running up and down the scale from one
note to another.

It was this howling and firing of the guns
at Ripley and St. George's Hill that we had
heard at Upper Halliford. The Ripley gunners,
unseasoned artillery volunteers who ought
never to have been placed in such a position,
fired one wild, premature, ineffectual volley,
and bolted on horse and foot through the deserted village, while the Martian, without using
his Heat Ray, walked serenely over their guns,
stepped gingerly among them, passed in front
of them, and so came unexpectedly upon the
guns in Painshill Park, which he destroyed.

The St. George's Hill men, however, were
better led or of a better mettle. Hidden by a
pine wood as they were, they seem to have
been quite unsuspected by the Martians nearest to them. They laid their guns as deliberately as if they had been on parade, and
fired at about a thousand-yard range.

The shells flashed all around him, and he
was seen to advance a few paces, stagger, and
go down. Everybody yelled together, and the
guns were reloaded in frantic haste. The overthrown Martian set up a prolonged ululation,
and immediately a second glittering giant,

answering him, appeared over the trees to the south. It would seem that a leg of the tripod had been smashed by one of the shells. The whole of the second volley flew wide of the Martian on the ground, and simultaneously, both his companions brought their Heat Rays to bear on the battery. The ammunition blew up, the pine trees all about the guns flashed into fire, and only one or two of the men who were already running over the crest of the hill escaped.

After this it would seem that the three took counsel together and halted, and the scouts who were watching them report that they remained absolutely stationary for the next half hour. The Martian who had been overthrown crawled tediously out of his hood, a small brown figure, oddly suggestive from that distance of a speck of blight, and apparently engaged in the repair of his support. About nine he had finished, for his cowl was then seen above the trees again.

It was a few minutes past nine that night when these three sentinels were joined by four other Martians, each carrying a thick black tube. A similar tube was handed to each of the three, and the seven proceeded to distribute themselves at equal distances along a curved line between St. George's Hill, Weybridge, and the village of Send, southwest of Ripley.

A dozen rockets sprang out of the hills before them so soon as they began to move, and

warned the waiting batteries about Ditton and
Esher. At the same time four of their fighting
machines, similarly armed with tubes, crossed
the river, and two of them, black against the
western sky, came into sight of myself and the
curate as we hurried wearily and painfully
along the road that runs northward out of
Halliford. They moved, as it seemed to us,
upon a cloud, for a milky mist covered the fields
and rose to a third of their height.

At this sight the curate cried faintly in his
throat, and began running; but I knew it was
no good running from a Martian, and I turned
aside and crawled through dewy nettles and
brambles into the broad ditch by the side of
the road. He looked back, saw what I was
doing, and turned to join me.

The two halted, the nearer to us standing
and facing Sunbury, the remoter being a gray
indistinctness toward the evening star, away
toward Staines.

The occasional howling of the Martians had
ceased; they took up their positions in the huge
crescent about their cylinders in absolute silence.
It was a crescent with twelve miles between its
horns. Never since the devising of gunpowder
was the beginning of a battle so still. To us
and to an observer about Ripley it would have
had precisely the same effect — the Martians
seemed in solitary possession of the darkling
night, lit only as it was by the slender moon,

the stars, the afterglow of the daylight, and
the ruddy glare from St. George's Hill and the
woods of Painshill.

But facing that crescent everywhere — at
Staines, Hounslow, Ditton, Esher, Ockham, behind hills and woods south of the river, and
across the flat grass meadows to the north of
it, wherever a cluster of trees or village houses
gave sufficient cover — the guns were waiting.
The signal rockets burst and rained their
sparks through the night and vanished, and
the spirit of all those watching batteries rose
to a tense expectation. The Martians had but
to advance into the line of fire, and instantly
those motionless black forms of men, those guns
glittering so darkly in the early night, would
explode into a thunderous fury of battle.

No doubt the thought that was uppermost in
a thousand of those vigilant minds, even as it
was uppermost in mine, was the riddle — how
much they understood of us. Did they grasp
that we in our millions were organized, disciplined, working together? Or did they interpret our spurts of fire, the sudden stinging of
our shells, our steady investment of their encampment, as we should the furious unanimity
of onslaught in a disturbed hive of bees? Did
they dream they might exterminate us? (At
that time no one knew what food they needed.)
A hundred such questions struggled together
in my mind as I watched that vast sentinel

shape. And in the back of my mind was the
sense of all the huge unknown and hidden
forces Londonward. Had they prepared pitfalls? Were the powder mills at Hounslow ready
as a snare? Would the Londoners have the
heart and courage to make a greater Moscow
of their mighty province of houses?

Then, after an interminable time, as it
seemed to us, crouching and peering through
the hedge, came a sound like the distant concussion of a gun. Another nearer, and then
another. And then the Martian beside us
raised his tube on high and discharged it, gun-
wise, with a heavy report that made the ground
heave. The one toward Staines answered him.
There was no flash, no smoke, simply that
loaded detonation.

I was so excited by these heavy minute guns
following one another that I so far forgot my
personal safety and my scalded hands as to
clamber up into the hedge and stare toward
Sunbury. As I did so a second report followed,
and a big projectile hurtled overhead toward
Hounslow. I expected at least to see smoke or
fire, or some such evidence of its work. But all
I saw was the deep-blue sky above, with one
solitary star, and the white mist spreading
wide and low beneath. And there had been no
crash, no answering explosion. The silence was
restored; the minute lengthened to three.

"What has happened?" said the curate, standing up beside me.

"Heaven knows!" said I.

A bat flickered by and vanished. A distant tumult of shouting began and ceased. I looked again at the Martian, and saw he was now moving eastward along the river bank, with a swift, rolling motion.

Every moment I expected the fire of some hidden battery to spring upon him; but the evening calm was unbroken. The figure of the Martian grew smaller as he receded, and presently the mist and the gathering night had swallowed him up. By a common impulse we clambered higher. Toward Sunbury was a dark appearance, as though a conical hill had suddenly come into being there, hiding our view of the farther country; and then, remoter across the river, over Walton, we saw another such summit. These hill-like forms grew lower and broader even as we stared.

Moved by a sudden thought, I looked northward, and there I perceived a third of these cloudy black kopjes had risen.

Everything had suddenly become very still. Far away to the southeast, marking the quiet, we heard the Martians hooting to one another, and then the air quivered again with the distant thud of their guns. But the earthly artillery made no reply.

Now at the time we could not understand

these things, but later I was to learn the meaning of these ominous kopjes that gathered in the twilight. Each of the Martians, standing in the great crescent I have described, had discharged, by means of the gunlike tube he carried, a huge canister over whatever hill, copse, cluster of houses, or other possible cover for guns, chanced to be in front of him. Some fired only one of these, some two — as in the case of the one we had seen; the one at Ripley is said to have discharged no fewer than five at that time. These canisters smashed on striking the ground — they did not explode — and incontinently disengaged an enormous volume of heavy, inky vapor, coiling and pouring upward in a huge and ebony cumulus cloud, a gaseous hill that sank and spread itself slowly over the surrounding country. And the touch of that vapor, the inhaling of its pungent wisps, was death to all that breathes.

It was heavy, this vapor, heavier than the densest smoke, so that, after the first tumultuous uprush and outflow of its impact, it sank down through the air and poured over the ground in a manner rather liquid than gaseous, abandoning the hills, and streaming into the valleys and ditches and watercourses even as I have heard the carbonic-acid gas that pours from volcanic clefts is wont to do. And where it came upon water some chemical action occurred, and the surface would be instantly

covered with a powdery scum that sank slowly
and made way for more. The scum was absolutely insoluble, and it is a strange thing,
seeing the instant effect of the gas, that one
could drink without hurt the water from which
it had been strained. The vapor did not diffuse
as a true gas would do. It hung together in
banks, flowing sluggishly down the slope of
the land and driving reluctantly before the
wind, and very slowly it combined with the mist
and moisture of the air, and sank to the earth
in the form of dust. Save that an unknown
element giving a group of four lines in the
blue of the spectrum is concerned, we are still
entirely ignorant of the nature of this sub-
stance.

Once the tumultuous upheaval of its disper-
sion was over, the black smoke clung so closely
to the ground, even before its precipitation,
that fifty feet up in the air, on the roofs and
upper stories of high houses and on great
trees, there was a chance of escaping its poison
altogether, as was proved even that night at
Street Cobham and Ditton.

The man who escaped at the former place
tells a wonderful story of the strangeness of
its coiling flow, and how he looked down from
the church spire and saw the houses of the
village rising like ghosts out of its inky noth-
ingness. For a day and a half he remained
there, weary, starving, and sun-scorched, the

earth under the blue sky and against the prospect of the distant hills a velvet-black expanse, with red roofs, green trees, and, later, black-veiled shrubs and gates, barns, outhouses, and walls, rising here and there into the sunlight.

But that was at Street Cobham, where the black vapor was allowed to remain until it sank of its own accord into the ground. As a rule the Martians, when it had served its purpose, cleared the air of it again by wading into it and directing a jet of steam upon it.

This they did with the vapor banks near us, as we saw in the starlight from the window of a deserted house at Upper Halliford, whither we had returned. From there we could see the searchlights on Richmond Hill and Kingston Hill going to and fro, and about eleven the windows rattled, and we heard the sound of the huge siege guns that had been put in position there. These continued intermittently for the space of a quarter of an hour, sending chance shots at the invisible Martians at Hampton and Ditton, and then the pale beams of the electric light vanished, and were replaced by a bright red glow.

Then the fourth cylinder fell — a brilliant green meteor — as I learned afterward, in Bushy Park. Before the guns on the Richmond and Kingston line of hills began, there was a fitful cannonade far away in the southwest, due, I believe, to guns being fired haphazard before the black vapor could overwhelm the gunners.

So, setting about it as methodically as men might smoke out a wasps' nest, the Martians spread this strange stifling vapor over the Londonward country. The horns of the crescent slowly moved apart, until at last they formed a line from Hanwell to Coombe and Malden. All night through their destructive tubes advanced. Never once, after the Martian at St. George's Hill was brought down, did they give the artillery the ghost of a chance against them. Whenever there was a possibility of guns being laid for them unseen, a fresh canister of the black vapor was discharged, and where the guns were openly displayed the Heat Ray was brought to bear:

By midnight the blazing trees along the slopes of Richmond Park and the glare of Kingston Hill threw their light upon a network of black smoke, blotting out the whole Valley of the Thames and extending as far as the eye could reach. And through this two Martians slowly waded, and turned their hissing steam jets this way and that.

They were sparing of the Heat Ray that night, either because they had but a limited supply of material for its production or because they did not wish to destroy the country but only to crush and overawe the opposition they had aroused. In the latter aim they certainly succeeded. Sunday night was the end of the organized opposition to their movements. After that no body of men would stand against them, so hopeless was the enterprise. Even the crews of the torpedo boats and destroyers that had brought their quick-firers up the Thames refused to stop, mutinied, and went down again. The only offensive operation men ventured upon after that night was the preparation of mines and pitfalls, and even in that their energies were frantic and spasmodic.

One has to imagine, as well as one may, the fate of those batteries toward Esher, waiting so tensely in the twilight. Survivors there were none. One may picture the orderly expectation, the officers alert and watchful, the gunners ready, the ammunition piled to hand, the limber gunners with their horses and wagons, the groups of civilian spectators standing as near as they were permitted, the evening stillness, the ambulances and hospital tents with the burned and wounded from Weybridge; then the dull resonance of the shots the Martians fired, and the clumsy projectile whirling over the trees and houses and smashing amid the neighboring fields.

One may picture, too, the sudden shifting of the attention, the swiftly spreading coils and bellyings of that blackness advancing headlong, towering heavenward, turning the twilight to a palpable darkness, a strange and horrible antagonist of vapor striding upon its victims, men and horses near it seen dimly, running, shrieking, falling headlong, shouts of dismay, the guns suddenly abandoned, men choking and writhing on the ground, and the swift broadening out of the opaque cone of smoke. And then night and extinction — nothing but a silent mass of impenetrable vapor hiding its dead.

Before dawn the black vapor was pouring through the streets of Richmond, and the disintegrating organism of government was, with a last expiring effort, rousing the population of London to the necessity of flight.

16. The Exodus from London

So you understand the roaring wave of fear that swept through the greatest city in the world just as Monday was dawning — the stream of flight rising swiftly to a torrent, lashing in a foaming tumult round the railway stations, banked up into a horrible struggle about the shipping in the Thames, and hurrying by every available channel northward and eastward. By ten o'clock the police organization, and by midday even the railway organizations, were losing coherency, losing shape and efficiency, guttering, softening, running at last in that swift liquefaction of the social body.

All the railway lines north of the Thames and the Southeastern people at Cannon Street had been warned by midnight on Sunday, and

trains were being filled. People were fighting
savagely for standing room in the carriages
even at two o'clock. By three, people were being
trampled and crushed even in Bishopsgate
Street, a couple of hundred yards or more
from Liverpool Street station; revolvers were
fired, people stabbed, and the policemen who
had been sent to direct the traffic, exhausted
and infuriated, were breaking the heads of
the people they were called out to protect.

And as the day advanced and the engine
drivers and stokers refused to return to London,
the pressure of the flight drove the people in an
ever-thickening multitude away from the stations and along the northward-running roads.
By midday a Martian had been seen at Barnes,
and a cloud of slowly sinking black vapor drove
along the Thames and across the flats of Lambeth, cutting off all escape over the bridges in
its sluggish advance. Another bank drove over
Ealing, and surrounded a little island of survivors on Castle Hill, alive, but unable to escape.

After a fruitless struggle to get aboard a
Northwestern train at Chalk Farm — the engines of the trains that had loaded in the
goods yard there *ploughed* through shrieking
people, and a dozen stalwart men fought to
keep the crowd from crushing the driver against
his furnace — my brother emerged upon the
Chalk Farm road, dodged across through a

hurrying swarm of vehicles, and had the luck
to be foremost in the sack of a cycle shop.
The front tire of the machine he got was punc-
tured in dragging it through the window, but
he got up and off, notwithstanding, with no
further injury than a cut wrist. The steep foot
of Haverstock Hill was impassable owing to
several overturned horses, and my brother
struck into Belsize Road.

So he got out of the fury of the panic, and,
skirting the Edgware Road, reached Edgware
about seven, fasting and wearied, but well
ahead of the crowd. Along the road people
were standing in the roadway, curious, wondering. He was passed by a number of cyclists,
some horsemen, and two motorcars. A mile
from Edgware the rim of the wheel broke, and
the machine became unridable. He left it by
the roadside and trudged through the village.
There were shops half opened in the main
street of the place, and people crowded on the
pavement and in the doorways and windows,
staring astonished at this extraordinary procession of fugitives that was beginning. He
succeeded in getting some food at an inn.

For a time he remained in Edgware not
knowing what next to do. The flying people
increased in number. Many of them, like my
brother, seemed inclined to loiter in the place.
There was no fresh news of the invaders from
Mars.

At that time the road was crowded, but as yet far from congested. Most of the fugitives at that hour were mounted on cycles, but there were soon motorcars, hansom cabs, and carriages hurrying along, and the dust hung in heavy clouds along the road to St. Albans.

It was perhaps a vague idea of making his way to Chelmsford, where some friends of his lived, that at last induced my brother to strike into a quiet lane running eastward. Presently he came upon a stile, and crossing it, followed a footpath northeastward. He passed near several farmhouses and some little places whose names he did not learn. He saw few fugitives until, in a grass lane toward High Barnet, he happened upon two ladies who became his fellow travelers. He came upon them just in time to save them.

He heard their screams, and, hurrying round the corner, saw a couple of men struggling to drag them out of the little pony chaise in which they had been driving, while a third with difficulty held the frightened pony's head. One of the ladies, a short woman dressed in white, was simply screaming; the other, a dark, slender figure, slashed at the man who gripped her arm with a whip she held in her disengaged hand.

My brother immediately grasped the situation, shouted, and hurried toward the struggle. One of the men desisted and turned toward

him, and my brother, realizing from his antagonist's face that a fight was unavoidable,
and being an expert boxer, went into him
forthwith and sent him down against the wheel
of the chaise.

It was no time for pugilistic chivalry and my
brother laid him quiet with a kick, and gripped
the collar of the man who pulled at the slender
lady's arm. He heard the clatter of hoofs, the
whip stung across his face, a third antagonist
struck him between the eyes, and the man he
held wrenched himself free and made off down
the lane in the direction from which he had
come.

Partly stunned, he found himself facing the
man who had held the horse's head, and became aware of the chaise receding from him
down the lane, swaying from side to side, and
with the women in it looking back. The man
before him, a burly rough, tried to close, and
he stopped him with a blow in the face. Then,
realizing that he was deserted, he dodged
round and made off down the lane after the
chaise, with the sturdy man close behind him,
and the fugitive, who had turned now, following remotely.

Suddenly he stumbled and fell; his immediate pursuer went headlong, and he rose to his
feet to find himself with a couple of antagonists
again. He would have had little chance against
them had not the slender lady very pluckily

pulled up and returned to his help. It seems she had a revolver all this time, but it had been under the seat when she and her companion were attacked. She fired at six yards' distance, narrowly missing my brother. The less courageous of the robbers made off, and his companion followed him, cursing his cowardice. They both stopped in sight down the lane where the third man lay insensible.

"Take this!" said the slender lady, and she gave my brother her revolver.

"Go back to the chaise," said my brother, wiping the blood from his split lip.

She turned without a word — they were both panting — and they went back to where the lady in white struggled to hold back the frightened pony.

The robbers had evidently had enough of it. When my brother looked again they were retreating.

"I'll sit here," said my brother, "if I may"; and he got upon the empty front seat. The lady looked over her shoulder.

"Give me the reins," she said, and laid the whip along the pony's side. In another moment a bend in the road hid the three men from my brother's eyes.

So, quite unexpectedly, my brother found himself, panting, with a cut mouth, a bruised jaw, and blood-stained knuckles, driving along an unknown lane with these two women.

He learned they were the wife and the
younger sister of a surgeon living at Stanmore, who had come in the small hours from a
dangerous case at Pinner, and heard at some
railway station on his way of the Martian advance. He had hurried home, roused the wom-
en — their servant had left them two days
before — packed some provisions, put his revolver under the seat — luckily for my brother
— and told them to drive on to Edgware, with
the idea of getting a train there. He stopped
behind to tell the neighbors. He would overtake them, he said, at about half-past four in
the morning, and now it was nearly nine and
they had seen nothing of him. They could not
stop in Edgware because of the growing traffic
through the place, and so they had come into
this side lane.

That was the story they told my brother in
fragments when presently they stopped again,
nearer to New Barnet. He promised to stay
with them, at least until they could determine
what to do, or until the missing man arrived,
and professed to be an expert shot with the
revolver — a weapon strange to him — in order to give them confidence.

They made a sort of encampment by the
wayside, and the pony became happy in the
hedge. He told them of his own escape out of
London, and all that he knew of these Martians
and their ways. The sun crept higher in the

sky, and after a time their talk died out and gave place to an uneasy state of anticipation. Several wayfarers came along the lane, and of these my brother gathered such news as he could. Every broken answer he had deepened his impression of the great disaster that had come on humanity, deepened his persuasion of the immediate necessity for prosecuting this flight. He urged the matter upon them.

"We have money," said the slender woman, and hesitated.

Her eyes met my brother's, and her hesitation ended.

"So have I," said my brother.

She explained that they had as much as thirty pounds in gold, besides a five-pound note, and suggested that with that they might get upon a train at St. Albans or New Barnet. My brother thought that was hopeless, seeing the fury of the Londoners to crowd upon the trains, and broached his own idea of striking across Essex toward Harwich and thence escaping from the country altogether.

Mrs. Elphinstone — that was the name of the woman in white — would listen to no reasoning, and kept calling upon "George"; but her sister-in-law was astonishingly quiet and deliberate, and at last agreed to my brother's suggestion. So, designing to cross the Great North Road, they went on toward Barnet, my brother leading the pony to save it as much as possible.

As the sun crept up the sky the day became excessively hot, and underfoot a thick, whitish sand grew burning and blinding, so that they traveled only very slowly. The hedges were gray with dust. And as they advanced toward Barnet a tumultuous murmuring grew stronger.

They began to meet more people. For the most part these were staring before them, murmuring indistinct questions, jaded, haggard, unclean. One man in evening dress passed them on foot, his eyes on the ground. They heard his voice, and, looking back at him saw one hand clutched in his hair and the other beating invisible things. His paroxysm of rage over, he went on his way without once looking back.

As my brother's party went on toward the crossroads to the south of Barnet they saw a woman approaching the road across some fields on their left, carrying a child and with two other children; and then passed a man in dirty black, with a thick stick in one hand and a small portmanteau in the other. Then round the corner of the lane, from between the villas that guarded it at its confluence with the highroad, came a little cart drawn by a sweating black pony and driven by a sallow youth in a bowler hat, gray with dust. There were three girls, East End factory girls, and a couple of little children crowded in the cart.

"This'll tike us rahnd Edgware?" asked the driver, wild-eyed, white-faced; and when my brother told him it would if he turned to the left, he whipped up at once without the formality of thanks.

My brother noticed a pale gray smoke or haze rising among the houses in front of them, and veiling the white-facade of a terrace beyond the road that appeared between the backs of the villas. Mrs. Elphinstone suddenly cried out at a number of tongues of smoky red flame leaping up above the houses in front of them against the hot, blue sky. The tumultuous noise resolved itself now into the disorderly mingling of many voices, the grind of many wheels, the creaking of wagons, and the staccato of hoofs. The lane came round sharply not fifty yards from the crossroads.

"Good heavens!" cried Mrs. Elphinstone. "What is this you are driving us into?"

My brother stopped.

For the main road was a boiling stream of people, a torrent of human beings rushing northward, one pressing on another. A great bank of dust, white and luminous in the blaze of the sun, made everything within twenty feet of the ground gray and indistinct and was perpetually renewed by the hurrying feet of a dense crowd of horses and women on foot, and by the wheels of vehicles of every description.

"Way!" my brother heard voices crying. "Make way!"

It was like riding into the smoke of a fire to approach the meeting point of the lane and road; the crowd roared like a fire, and the dust was hot and pungent. And, indeed, a little way up the road a villa was burning and sending rolling masses of black smoke across the road to add to the confusion.

Two men came past them. Then a dirty woman, carrying a heavy bundle and weeping. A lost retriever dog, with hanging tongue, circled dubiously round them, scared and wretched, and fled at my brother's threat.

So much as they could see of the road Londonward between the houses to the right was a tumultuous stream of dirty, hurrying people, pent in between the villas on either side; the black heads, the crowded forms, grew into distinctness as they rushed toward the corner, hurried past, and merged their individuality again in a receding multitude that was swallowed up at last in a cloud of dust.

"Go on! Go on!" cried the voices. "Way! Way!"

One man's hands pressed on the back of another. My brother stood at the pony's head. Irresistibly attracted, he advanced slowly pace by pace, down the lane.

Edgware had been a scene of confusion, Chalk Farm a riotous tumult, but this was a whole population in movement. It is hard to imagine that host. It had no character of its own. The figures poured out past the corner, and receded with their backs to the group in the lane. Along the margin came those who were on foot threatened by the wheels, stumbling in the ditches, blundering into one another.

The carts and carriages crowded close upon one another, making little way for those swifter and more impatient vehicles that darted forward every now and then when an opportunity showed itself of doing so, sending the people scattering against the fences and gates of the villas.

"Push on" was the cry. "Push on! They are coming!"

In one cart stood a blind man in the uniform of the Salvation Army, gesticulating with his crooked fingers and bawling, "Eternity! Eternity!" His voice was hoarse and very loud so that my brother could hear him long after he was lost to sight in the dust. Some of the people who crowded in the carts whipped stupidly at their horses and quarreled with other drivers; some sat motionless, staring at nothing with miserable eyes; some gnawed their hands with thirst, or lay prostrate in the bottoms of their conveyances. The horses' bits were covered with foam, their eyes bloodshot.

There were cabs, carriages, shop carts, wagons, beyond counting; a mail cart, a road-cleaner's cart marked "Vestry of St. Pancras," a huge timber wagon crowded with roughs. A brewer's dray rumbled by with its two near wheels splashed with fresh blood.

"Clear the way!" cried the voices. "Clear the way!"

"Eter-nity! Eter-nity!" came echoing down the road.

There were sad, haggard women tramping by, well-dressed, with children that cried and stumbled, their dainty clothes smothered in dust, their weary faces smeared with tears. With many of these came men, sometimes helpful, sometimes lowering and savage. Fighting side by side with them pushed some weary street outcast in faded black rags, wide-eyed, loud-voiced, and foul-mouthed. There were sturdy workmen thrusting their way along, wretched, unkempt men, clothed like clerks or shop men, struggling spasmodically; a wounded soldier my brother noticed, men dressed in the clothes of railway porters, one wretched creature in a nightshirt with a coat thrown over it.

But varied as its composition was, certain things all that host had in common. There were fear and pain on their faces, and fear behind them. A tumult up the road, a quarrel for a place in a wagon, sent the whole host of them quickening their pace; even a man so scared and broken that his knees bent under him was galvanized for a moment into renewed activity.

The heat and dust had already been at work upon this multitude. Their skins were dry, their lips black and cracked. They were all thirsty, weary, and footsore. And amid the various cries one heard disputes, reproaches, groans of weariness, and fatigue; the voices of most of them were hoarse and weak. Through it all ran a refrain:

"Way! Way! The Martians are coming!"

Few stopped and came aside from that flood. The lane opened slantingly into the main road with a narrow opening, and had a delusive appearance of coming from the direction of London. Yet a kind of eddy of people drove into its mouth; weaklings elbowed out of the stream, who for the most part rested but a moment before plunging into it again. A little way down the lane, with two friends bending over him, lay a man with a bare leg, wrapped about with bloody rags. He was a lucky man to have friends.

A little old man, with a gray military mustache and a filthy black frock coat, limped out and sat down beside the trap, removed his boot — his sock was bloodstained — shook out a pebble, and hobbled on again; and then a little girl of eight or nine, all alone, threw herself under the hedge close by my brother, weeping.

"I can't go on! I can't go on!"

My brother woke from his torpor of astonishment and lifted her up, speaking gently to her,

and carried her to Miss Elphinstone. So soon
as my brother touched her she became quite
still, as if frightened.

"Ellen!" shrieked a woman in the crowd, with
tears in her voice — "Ellen!" And the child
suddenly darted away from my brother, crying, "Mother!"

"They are coming," said a man on horseback,
riding past along the lane.

"Out of the way, there!" bawled a coach-
man, towering high; and my brother saw a
closed carriage turning into the lane.

The people crushed back on one another to
avoid the horse. My brother pushed the pony
and chaise back into the hedge, and the man
drove by and stopped at the turn of the way. It
was a carriage, with a pole for a pair of horses,
but only one was in the traces. My brother saw
dimly through the dust that two men lifted out
something on a white stretcher and put it gently
on the grass beneath the privet hedge.

One of the men came running to my brother.
"Where is there any water?" he said. "He
is dying fast, and very thirsty. It is Lord Garrick."

"Lord Garrick!" said my brother — "the
Chief Justice?"

"The water?" he said.

"There may be a tap," said my brother, "in
some of the houses. We have no water. I dare
not leave my people."

The man pushed against the crowd toward the gate of the corner house.

"Go on!" said the people, thrusting at him. "They are coming! Go on!"

Then my brother's attention was distracted by a bearded, eagle-faced man lugging a small handbag, which split even as my brother's eyes rested on it and disgorged a mass of sovereigns that seemed to break up into separate coins as it struck the ground. They rolled hither and thither among the struggling feet of men and horses. The man stopped and looked stupidly at the heap, and the shaft of a cab struck his shoulder and sent him wheeling. He gave a shriek and dodged back, and a cartwheel shaved him narrowly.

"Way!" cried the men all about him. "Make way!"

Soon as the cab had passed, he flung himself, with both hands open, upon the heap of coins, and began thrusting handfuls in his pocket. A horse rose close upon him, and in another moment, half rising, he had been borne down under the horse's hoofs.

"Stop!" screamed my brother, and pushing a woman out of his way, tried to clutch the bit of the horse.

Before he could get to it, he heard a scream under the wheels, and saw through the dust the rim passing over the poor wretch's back. The driver of the cart slashed his whip at my

brother, who ran round behind the cart. The
multitudinous shouting confused his ears. The
man was writhing in the dust among his scattered money, unable to rise, for the wheel had
broken his back, and his lower limbs lay limp
and dead. My brother stood up and yelled at
the next driver, and a man on a black horse
came to his assistance.

"Get him out of the road," said he; and,
clutching the man's collar with his free hand,
my brother lugged him sideways. But he still
clutched after his money, and regarded my
brother fiercely, hammering at his arm with a
handful of gold. "Go on! Go on!" shouted angry voices behind. "Way! Way!"

There was a smash as the pole of a carriage
crashed into the cart that the man on horseback
stopped. My brother looked up, and the man
with the gold twisted his head round and bit
the wrist that held his collar. There was a
concussion, and the black horse came staggering
sideways, and the cart-horse pulled beside it. A
hoof missed my brother's foot by a hair's
breadth. He released his grip on the fallen
man and jumped back. He saw anger change to
terror on the face of the poor wretch on the
ground, and in a moment he was hidden and
my brother was borne backward and carried
past the entrance of the lane, and had to fight
hard in the torrent to recover it.

He saw Miss Elphinstone covering her eyes,

and a little child, with all a child's want of
sympathetic imagination, staring with dilated
eyes at a dusty something that lay black and
still, ground and crushed under the rolling
wheels. "Let us go back!" he shouted, and began turning the pony round. "We cannot cross
this — hell," he said; and they went back a
hundred yards the way they had come, until
the fighting crowd was hidden. As they passed
the bend in the lane my brother saw the face
of the dying man in the ditch under the privet,
deadly white and drawn, and shining with
perspiration. The two women sat silent, crouching in their seat and shivering.

Then beyond the bend my brother stopped
again. Miss Elphinstone was white and pale,
too wretched even to call upon "George," and
her sister-in-law sat weeping. My brother was
horrified and perplexed. So soon as they had
retreated he realized how urgent and unavoidable it was to attempt this crossing. He turned
to Miss Elphinstone, suddenly resolute.

"We must go that way," he said, and led
the pony round again.

For the second time that day this girl proved
her quality. To force their way into the torrent
of people, my brother plunged into the traffic
and held back a cab horse, while she drove the
pony across its head. A wagon locked wheels
for a moment and ripped a long splinter from
the chaise. In another moment they were caught

and swept forward by the stream. My brother, with the cabman's whip marks red across his face and hands, scrambled into the chaise and took the reins from her.

"Point the revolver at the man behind," he said, giving it to her, "if he presses us too hard. No — point it at his horse!"

Then he began to look out for a chance of edging to the right across the road. But once in the stream he seemed to lose volition, to become a part of that dusty rout. They swept through Chipping Barnet with the torrent; they were nearly a mile beyond the center of the town before they had fought across to the opposite side of the way. It was din and confusion indescribable; but in and beyond the town the road forks repeatedly, and this to some extent relieved the stress.

They struck eastward through Hadley, and there on either side of the road, and at another place farther on they came upon a great multitude of people drinking at the stream, some fighting to come at the water. And farther on, from a hill near East Barnet, they saw two trains running slowly one after the other without signal or order — trains swarming with people, with men even among the coals behind the engines — going northward along the Great Northern Railway. My brother supposes they must have filled outside London, for at that time the furious terror of the people had rendered the central termini impossible.

Near this place they halted for the rest of the afternoon, for the violence of the day had already utterly exhausted all three of them. They began to suffer the beginnings of hunger; the night was cold, and none of them dared to sleep. And in the evening many people came hurrying along the road near by their stopping place, fleeing from unknown dangers before them, and going in the direction from which my brother had come.

17. The "Thunder Child"

HAD THE MARTIANS aimed only at destruction, they might on Monday have annihilated the entire population of London, as it spread itself slowly through the home countries. Not only along the road through Barnet, but also through Edgware and Waltham Abbey, and along the roads eastward to Southend and Shoeburyness, and south of the Thames to Deal and Broadstairs, poured the same frantic rout. If one could have hung that June morning in a balloon in the blazing blue above London every northward and eastward road running out of the tangled maze of streets would have seemed stippled black with the streaming fugitives, each dot a human agony of terror and physical distress. I have set forth at length

in the last chapter my brother's account of
the road through Chipping Barnet, in order
that my readers may realize how that swarming of black dots appeared to one of those concerned. Never before in the history of the
world had such a mass of human beings moved
and suffered together. The legendary hosts of
Goths and Huns, the hugest armies Asia has
ever seen, would have been but a drop in
that current. And this was no disciplined
march; it was a stampede — a stampede gigantic and terrible — without order and without a goal, six million people, unarmed and
unprovisioned, driving headlong. It was the
beginning of the rout of civilization, of the
massacre of mankind.

Directly below him the balloonist would
have seen the network of streets far and wide,
houses, churches, squares, crescents, gardens
— already derelict — spread out like a huge
map, and in the southward *blotted*. Over Ealing, Richmond, Wimbledon, it would have
seemed as if some monstrous pen had flung ink
upon the chart. Steadily, incessantly, each
black splash grew and spread, shooting out
ramifications this way and that, now banking itself against rising ground, now pouring swiftly
over a crest into a new-found valley, exactly as
a gout of ink would spread itself upon blotting
paper.

And beyond, over the blue hills that rise

southward of the river, the glittering Martians went to and fro, calmly and methodically spreading their poison cloud over this patch of country and then over that, laying it again with their steam jets when it had served its purpose, and taking possession of the conquered country. They do not seem to have aimed at extermination so much as at complete demoralization and the destruction of any opposition. They exploded any stores of powder they came upon, cut every telegraph, and wrecked the railways here and there. They were hamstringing mankind. They seemed in no hurry to extend the field of their operations, and did not come beyond the central part of London all that day. It is possible that a very considerable number of people in London stuck to their houses through Monday morning. Certain it is that many died at home suffocated by the Black Smoke.

Until about midday the Pool of London was an astonishing scene. Steamboats and shipping of all sorts lay there, tempted by the enormous sums of money offered by fugitives, and it is said that many who swam out to these vessels were thrust off with boat hooks and drowned. About one o'clock in the afternoon the thinning remnant of a cloud of the black vapor appeared between the arches of Blackfriars Bridge. At that the Pool became a scene of mad confusion, fighting, and collision, and for some time a multitude of boats and barges jammed in the northern arch of the Tower Bridge, and the sailors and lightermen had to fight savagely against the people who swarmed upon them from the river front. People were actually clambering down the piers of the bridge from above.

When, an hour later, a Martian appeared beyond the Clock Tower and waded down the river, nothing but wreckage floated above Limehouse.

Of the falling of the fifth cylinder I have presently to tell. The sixth star fell at Wimbledon. My brother, keeping watch beside the women in the chaise in a meadow, saw the green flash of it far beyond the hills. On Tuesday the little party, still set upon getting across the sea, made its way through the swarming country toward Colchester. The news that the Martians were now in possession of the whole of London was confirmed. They had been seen at Highgate, and even, it was said, at Neasden. But they did not come into my brother's view until the morrow.

That day the scattered multitudes began to realize the urgent need of provisions. As they grew hungry the rights of property ceased to be regarded. Farmers were out to defend their cattle sheds, granaries, and ripening root crops with arms in their hands. A number of people now, like my brother, had their faces eastward, and there were some desperate souls even going back toward London to get food. These were chiefly people from the northern suburbs, whose knowledge of the Black Smoke came by hearsay. He heard that about half the members of the government had gathered at Birmingham, and that enormous quantities of high explosives were being prepared to be used in automatic mines across the Midland countries.

He was also told that the Midland Railway Company had replaced the desertions of the first day's panic, had resumed traffic, and was running northward trains from St. Albans to relieve the congestion of the home counties. There was also a placard in Chipping Ongar announcing that large stores of flour were available in the northern towns and that within twenty-four hours bread would be distributed among the starving people in the neighborhood. But this intelligence did not deter him from the plan of escape he had formed, and the three pressed eastward all day, and heard no more of the bread distribution than this promise. Nor, as a matter of fact, did anyone else hear more of it. That night fell the seventh star, falling upon Primrose Hill. It fell while Miss Elphinstone was watching, for she took that duty alternately with my brother. She saw it.

On Wednesday the three fugitives — they had passed the night in a field of unripe wheat

— reached Chelmsford, and there a body of the inhabitants, calling itself the Committee of Public Supply, seized the pony as provisions, and would give nothing in exchange for it but the promise of a share in it the next day. Here there were rumors of Martians at Epping, and news of the destruction of Waltham Abbey Powder Mills in a vain attempt to blow up one of the invaders.

People were watching for Martians here from the church towers. My brother, very luckily for him as it chanced, preferred to push on at once to the coast rather than wait for food, although all three of them were very hungry. By midday they passed through Tillingham, which, strangely enough, seemed to be quite silent and deserted, save for a few furtive plunderers hunting for food. Near Tillingham they suddenly came in sight of the sea, and the most amazing crowd of shipping of all sorts that it is possible to imagine.

For after the sailors could no longer come up the Thames, they came on to the Essex coast, to Harwich and Walton and Clacton, and afterward to Foulness and Shoebury, to bring off the people. They lay in a huge sickle-shaped curve that vanished into mist at last toward the Naze. Close inshore was a multitude of fishing smacks — English, Scotch, French, Dutch, and Swedish; steam launches from the Thames, yachts, electric boats; and beyond were ships of large burden, a multitude of filthy colliers, trim merchantmen, cattle ships, passenger boats, petroleum tanks, ocean tramps, an old white transport even, neat white and gray liners from Southampton and Hamburg; and long the blue coast across the Blackwater my brother could make out dimly a dense swarm of boats chaffering with the people on the beach, a swarm which also extended up the Blackwater almost to Maldon.

About a couple of miles out lay an ironclad, very low in the water, almost, to my brother's perception, like a water-logged ship. This was the ram *Thunder Child*. It was the only warship in sight, but far away to the right over the smooth surface of the sea — for that day there was a dead calm — lay a serpent of black smoke to mark the next ironclads of the Channel Fleet, which hovered in an extended line, steam up and ready for action, across the Thames estuary during the course of the Martian conquest vigilant and yet powerless to prevent it.

At the sight of the sea, Mrs. Elphinstone, in spite of the assurances of her sister-in-law, gave way to panic. She had never been out of England before, she would rather die than trust herself friendless in a foreign country, and so forth. She seemed, poor woman, to imagine that the French and the Martians might prove very similar. She had been growing increasingly hysterical, fearful, and depressed during the

two days' journeyings. Her great idea was to return to Stanmore. Things had been always well
and safe at Stanmore. They would find George
at Stanmore.

It was with the greatest difficulty they could
get her down to the beach, where presently my
brother succeeded in attracting the attention
of some men on a paddle steamer from the
Thames. They sent a boat and drove a bargain
for thirty-six pounds for the three. The steamer
was going, these men said, to Ostend.

It was about two o'clock when my brother,
having paid their fares at the gangway, found
himself safely aboard the steamboat with his
charges. There was food aboard, albeit at ex-
orbitant prices, and the three of them contrived
to eat a meal on one of the seats forward.

There were already a couple of score of passengers aboard, some of whom had expended
their last money in securing a passage, but the
captain lay off the Blackwater until five in the
afternoon, picking up passengers until the
seated decks were even dangerously crowded.
He would probably have remained longer had it
not been for the sound of guns that began about
that hour in the south. As if in answer, the ironclad seaward fired a small gun and hoisted a
string of flags. A jet of smoke sprang out of her
funnels.

Some of the passengers were of opinion that
this firing came from Shoeburyness, until it

was noticed that it was growing louder. At the same time, far away in the southeast the masts and upper works of three ironclads rose one after the other out of the sea, beneath clouds of black smoke. But my brother's attention speedily reverted to the distant firing in the south. He fancied he saw a column of smoke rising out of the distant gray haze.

The little steamer was already flapping her way eastward of the big crescent of shipping, and the low Essex coast was growing blue and hazy, when a Martian appeared, small and faint in the remote distance, advancing along the muddy coast from the direction of Foulness. At that the captain on the bridge swore at the top of his voice with fear and anger at his own delay, and the paddles seemed infected with his terror. Every soul aboard stood at the bulwarks or on the seats of the steamer and stared at that distant shape, higher than the trees or church towers inland, and advancing with a leisurely parody of a human stride.

It was the first Martian my brother had seen, and he stood, more amazed than terrified, watching this Titan advancing deliberately toward the shipping, wading farther and farther into the water as the coast fell away. Then, far away beyond the Crouch, came another, striding over some stunted trees, and then yet another, still farther off, wading deeply through a shiny mudflat that seemed to hang halfway

up between sea and sky. They were all stalking
seaward, as if to intercept the escape of the
multitudinous vessels that were crowded between Foulness and the Naze. In spite of the
throbbing exertions of the engines of the little
paddle boat, and the pouring foam that her
wheels flung behind her, she receded with ter-
rifying slowness from this ominous advance.

Glancing northwestward, my brother saw the
large crescent of shipping already writhing
with the approaching terror; one ship passing
behind another, another coming round from
broadside to end on, steamships whistling and
giving off volumes of steam, sails being let out,
launches rushing hither and thither. He was so
fascinated by this and by the creeping danger
away to the left that he had no eyes for anything seaward. And then a swift movement of
the steamboat (she had suddenly come round
to avoid being run down) flung him headlong
from the seat upon which he was standing.
There was a shouting all about him, a trampling
of feet, and a cheer that seemed to be answered
faintly. The steamboat lurched and rolled him
over upon his hands.

He sprang to his feet and saw to starboard,
and not a hundred yards from their heeling,
pitching boat, a vast iron bulk like the blade
of a plough tearing through the water, tossing
it on either side in huge waves of foam that
leaped toward the steamer, flinging her paddles

helplessly in the air, and then sucking her deck down almost to the waterline.

A douche of spray blinded my brother for a moment. When his eyes were clear again he saw the monster had passed and was rushing landward. Big iron upperworks rose out of this headlong structure, and from that twin funnels projected and spat a smoking blast shot with fire. It was the torpedo ram, *Thunder Child*, steaming headlong, coming to the rescue of the threatened shipping.

Keeping his footing on the heaving deck by clutching the bulwarks, my brother looked past this charging leviathan at the Martians again, and he saw the three of them now close together, and standing so far out to sea that their tripod supports were almost entirely submerged. Thus sunken, and seen in remote perspective, they appeared far less formidable than the huge iron bulk in whose wake the steamer was pitching so helplessly. It would seem they were regarding this new antagonist with astonishment. To their intelligence, it may be, the giant was even such another as themselves. The *Thunder Child* fired no gun, but simply drove full speed toward them. It was probably her not firing that enabled her to get so near the enemy as she did. They did not know what to make of her. One shell, and they would have sent her to the bottom forthwith with the Heat Ray.

She was steaming at such a pace that in a minute she seemed halfway between the steamboat and the Martians — a diminishing black bulk against the receding horizontal expanse of the Essex coast.

Suddenly the foremost Martian lowered his tube and discharged a canister of the black gas at the ironclad. It hit her larboard side and glanced off in an inky jet that rolled away to seaward, an unfolding torrent of Black Smoke, from which the ironclad drove clear. To the watchers from the steamer, low in the water and with the sun in their eyes, it seemed as though she were already among the Martians.

They saw the gaunt figures separating and rising out of the water as they retreated shoreward, and one of them raised the cameralike generator of the Heat Ray. He held it pointing obliquely downward, and a bank of steam sprang from the water at its touch. It must have driven through the iron of the ship's side like a white-hot iron rod through paper.

A flicker of flame went up through the rising steam, and then the Martian reeled and staggered. In another moment he was cut down, and a great body of water and steam shot high in the air. The guns of the *Thunder Child* sounded through the reek, going off one after the other, and one shot splashed the water high close by the steamer, ricocheted toward the other flying ships to the north, and smashed a smack to matchwood.

But no one heeded that very much. At the sight of the Martian's collapse the captain on the bridge yelled inarticulately, and all the crowding passengers on the steamer's stern shouted together. And then they yelled again. For, surging out beyond the white tumult drove something long and black, the flames streaming from its middle parts, its ventilators and funnels spouting fire.

She was alive still; the steering gear, it seems, was intact and her engines working. She headed straight for a second Martian, and was within a hundred yards of him when the Heat Ray came to bear. Then with a violent thud, a blinding flash, her decks, her funnels, leaped upward. The Martian staggered with the violence of her explosion, and in another moment the flaming wreckage, still driving forward with the impetus of its pace, had struck him and crumpled him up like a thing of cardboard. My brother shouted involuntarily. A boiling tumult of steam hid everything again.

"Two!" yelled the captain.

Everyone was shouting. The whole steamer from end to end rang with frantic cheering that was taken up first by one and then by all in the crowding multitude of ships and boats that was driving out to sea.

The steam hung upon the water for many

minutes, hiding the third Martian and the coast altogether. And all this time the boat was paddling steadily out to sea and away from the fight; and when at last the confusion cleared, the drifting bank of black vapor intervened, and nothing of the *Thunder Child* could be made out, nor could the third Martian be seen. But the ironclads to seaward were now quite close and standing in toward shore past the steamboat.

The little vessel continued to beat its way seaward, and the ironclads receded slowly toward the coast, which was hidden still by a marbled bank of vapor, part steam, part black gas, eddying and combining in the strangest way. The fleet of refugees was scattering to the northeast; several smacks were sailing between the ironclads and the steamboat. After a time, and before they reached the sinking cloud bank, the warships turned northward, and then abruptly went about and passed into the thickening haze of evening southward. The coast grew faint, and at last indistinguishable amid the low banks of clouds that were gathering about the sinking sun.

Then suddenly out of the golden haze of the sunset came the vibration of guns, and a form of black shadows moving. Everyone struggled to the rail of the steamer and peered into the blinding furnace of the west, but nothing was to be distinguished clearly. A mass of smoke rose slanting and barred the face of the sun. The steamboat throbbed on its way through an interminable suspense.

The sun sank into gray clouds, the sky flushed and darkened, the evening star trembled into sight. It was deep twilight when the captain cried out and pointed. My brother strained his eyes. Something rushed up into the sky out of the grayness — rushed slantingly upward and very swiftly into the luminous clearness above the clouds in the western sky; something flat and broad and very large, that swept round in a vast curve, grew smaller, sank slowly, and vanished again into the gray mystery of the night. And as it flew it rained down darkness upon the land.

Book II
THE EARTH
UNDER THE MARTIANS

1. Under Foot

IN THE FIRST BOOK I have wandered so much
from my own adventures to tell of the experiences of my brother that all through the last
two chapters I and the curate have been lurking
in the empty house at Halliford whither we fled
to escape the Black Smoke. There I will resume.
We stopped there all Sunday night and all the
next day — the day of the panic — in a little
island of daylight, cut off by the Black Smoke
from the rest of the world. We could do nothing
but wait in aching inactivity during those two
weary days.

My mind was occupied by anxiety for my
wife. I figured her at Leatherhead, terrified, in
danger, mourning me already as a dead man. I
paced the rooms and cried aloud when I thought

of how I was cut off from her, of all that might happen to her in my absence. My cousin I knew was brave enough for any emergency, but he was not the sort of man to realize danger quickly, to rise promptly. What was needed now was not bravery, but circumspection. My only consolation was to believe that the Martians were moving Londonward and away from her. Such vague anxieties keep the mind sensitive and painful. I grew very weary and irritable with the curate's perpetual ejaculations; I tired of the sight of his selfish despair. After some ineffectual remonstrance I kept away from him, staying in a room — evidently a children's schoolroom — containing globes, forms, and copy books. When he followed me thither, I went to a box room at the top of the house and, in order to be alone with my aching miseries, locked myself in.

We were hopelessly hemmed in by the Black Smoke all that day and the morning of the next. There were signs of people in the next house on Sunday evening — a face at a window and moving lights, and later the slamming of a door. But I do not know who these people were, nor what became of them. We saw nothing of them next day. The Black Smoke drifted slowly riverward all through Monday morning, creeping nearer and nearer to us, driving at last along the roadway outside the house that hid us.

A Martian came across the fields about mid-day, laying the stuff with a jet of superheated steam that hissed against the walls, smashed all the windows it touched, and scalded the curate's hand as he fled out of the front room. When at last we crept across the sodden rooms and looked out again, the country northward was as though a black snowstorm had passed over it. Looking toward the river, we were astonished to see an unaccountable redness mingling with the black of the scorched meadows.

For a time we did not see how this change affected our position, save that we were relieved of our fear of the Black Smoke. But later I perceived that we were no longer hemmed in, that now we might get away. As soon as I realized that the way of escape was open, my dream of action returned. But the curate was lethargic, unreasonable.

"We are safe here," he repeated; "safe here."

I resolved to leave him — would that I had! Wiser now for the artilleryman's teaching, I sought out food and drink. I had found oil and rags for my burns, and I also took a hat and a flannel shirt that I found in one of the bedrooms. When it was clear to him that I meant to go alone — had reconciled myself to going alone — he suddenly roused himself to come. And all being quiet throughout the afternoon, we started about five o'clock, as I should judge, along the blackened road to Sunbury.

In Sunbury, and at intervals along the road, were dead bodies lying in contorted attitudes, horses as well as men, overturned carts and luggage, all covered thickly with black dust. That pall of cindery powder made me think of what I had read of the destruction of Pompeii. We got to Hampton Court without misadventure, our minds full of strange and unfamiliar appearances, and at Hampton Court our eyes were relieved to find a patch of green that had escaped the suffocating drift. We went through Bushey Park, with its deer going to and fro under the chestnuts, and some men and women hurrying in the distance toward Hampton, and so we came to Twickenham. These were the first people we saw.

Away across the road the woods beyond Ham and Petersham were still afire. Twickenham was uninjured by either Heat Ray or Black Smoke, and there were more people about here, though none could give us news. For the most part they were like ourselves, taking advantage of a lull to shift their quarters. I have an impression that many of the houses here were still occupied by scared inhabitants, too frightened even for flight. Here, too, the evidence of a hasty rout was abundant along the road. I remember most vividly three smashed bicycles in a heap, pounded into the road by the wheels of subsequent carts. We crossed Richmond Bridge about half-past eight. We hurried across the exposed bridge, of course, but I noticed floating down the stream a number of red masses, some many feet across. I did not know what these were — there was no time for scrutiny — and I put a more horrible interpretation on them than they deserved. Here again on the Surrey side were black dust that had once been smoke, and dead bodies — a heap near the approach to the station; but we had no glimpse of the Martians until we were some way toward Barnes.

We saw in the blackened distance a group of three people running down a side street toward the river, but otherwise it seemed deserted. Up the hill Richmond town was burning briskly; outside the town of Richmond there was no trace of the Black Smoke.

Then suddenly, as we approached Kew, came a number of people running, and the upper works of a Martian fighting machine loomed in sight over the housetops, not a hundred yards away from us. We stood aghast at our danger, and had the Martian looked down we must immediately have perished. We were so terrified that we dared not go on, but turned aside and hid in a shed in a garden. There the curate crouched, weeping silently, and refusing to stir again.

But my fixed idea of reaching Leatherhead would not let me rest, and in the twilight I ventured out again. I went through a shrubbery, and along a passage beside a big house standing in its own grounds, and so emerged upon the road toward Kew. The curate I left in the shed, but he came hurrying after me.

That second start was the most foolhardy thing I ever did. For it was manifest the Martians were about us. No sooner had the curate overtaken me than we saw either the fighting machine we had seen before or another, far away across the meadows in the direction of Kew Lodge. Four or five little black figures hurried before it across the green-gray of the field, and in a moment it was evident this Martian pursued them. In three strides he was among them, and they ran radiating from his feet in all directions. He used no Heat Ray to destroy them, but picked them up one by one. Apparently he tossed them into the great metallic carrier which projected behind him, much as a workman's basket hangs over his shoulder.

It was the first time I realized that the Martians might have any other purpose than destruction with defeated humanity. We stood for a moment petrified, then turned and fled through a gate behind us into a walled garden, fell into, rather than found, a fortunate ditch, and lay there, scarce daring to whisper to each other until the stars were out.

I suppose it was nearly eleven o'clock before

we gathered courage to start again, no longer
venturing into the road, but sneaking along
hedgerows and through plantations, and watching keenly through the darkness, he on the
right and I on the left, for the Martians, who
seemed to be all about us. In one place we blundered upon a scorched and blackened area, now
cooling and ashen, and a number of scattered
dead bodies of men, burned horribly about the
heads and trunks but with their legs and boots ·
mostly intact; and of dead horses, fifty feet,
perhaps, behind a line of four ripped guns and
smashed gun carriages.

Sheen, it seemed, had escaped destruction,
but the place was silent and deserted. Here we
happened on no dead, though the night was too
dark for us to see into the side roads of the
place. In Sheen my companion suddenly com-
plained of faintness and thirst, and we decided
to try one of the houses.

The first house we entered, after a little difficulty with the window, was a small semide-
tached villa, and I found nothing eatable left in
the place but some moldy cheese. There was,
however, water to drink; and I took a hatchet,
which promised to be useful in our next house-
breaking.

We then crossed to a place where the road
turns toward Mortlake. Here there stood a
white house within a walled garden, and in the

pantry of this domicile we found a store of food
— two loaves of bread in a pan, an uncooked
steak, and the half of a ham. I give this cata-
logue so precisely because, as it happened, we
were destined to subsist upon this store for the
next fortnight. Bottled beer stood under a
shelf, and there were two bags of haricot beans
and some limp lettuces. This pantry opened into
a kind of washup kitchen, and in this was firewood; there was also a cupboard, in which we
found nearly a dozen of burgundy, tinned soups
and salmon, and two tins of biscuits.

We sat in the adjacent kitchen in the dark —
for we dared not strike a light — and ate bread
and ham, and drank beer out of the same bottle.
The curate, who was still timorous and restless,
was now, oddly enough, for pushing on, and
I was urging him to keep up his strength by
eating when the thing happened that was to
imprison us.

"It can't be midnight yet," I said, and then
came a blinding glare of vivid green light. Everything in the kitchen leaped out, clearly visible in green and black, and vanished again.
And then followed such a concussion as I have
never heard before or since. So close on the
heels of this as to seem instantaneous came a
thud behind me, a clash of glass, a crash and
rattle of falling masonry all about us, and the
plaster of the ceiling came down upon us,

smashing into a multitude of fragments upon
our heads. I was knocked headlong across the
floor against the oven handle and stunned. I
was insensible for a long time, the curate told
me, and when I came to we were in darkness
again, and he, with a face wet, as I found afterward, with blood from a cut forehead, was dab-
bing water over me.

For some time I could not recollect what had
happened. Then things came to me slowly. A
bruise on my temple asserted itself.

"Are you better?" asked the curate, in a
whisper.

At last I answered him. I sat up.

"Don't move," he said. "The floor is covered
with smashed crockery from the dresser. You
can't possibly move without making a noise,
and I fancy *they* are outside."

We both sat quite silent, so that we could
scarcely hear each other breathing. Everything
seemed deadly still, but once something near
us, some plaster or broken brickwork, slid down
with a rumbling sound. Outside and very near
was an intermittent, metallic rattle.

"That!" said the curate, when presently it
happened again.

"Yes," I said. "But what is it?"

"A Martian!" said the curate.

I listened again.

"It was not like the Heat Ray," I said, and for

a time I was inclined to think one of the great fighting machines had stumbled against the house, as I had seen one stumble against the tower of Shepperton Church.

Our situation was so strange and incomprehensible that for three or four hours, until the dawn came, we scarcely moved. And then the light filtered in, not through the window, which remained black, but through a triangular aperture between a beam and a heap of broken bricks in the wall behind us. The interior of the kitchen we now saw grayly for the first time.

The window had been burst in by a mass of garden mold, which flowed over the table upon which we had been sitting and lay about our feet. Outside, the soil was banked high against the house. At the top of the window frame we could see an uprooted drainpipe. The floor was littered with smashed hardware; the end of the kitchen toward the house was broken into, and since the daylight shone in there, it was evident the greater part of the house had collapsed. Contrasting vividly with this ruin was the neat dresser, stained in the fashion, pale green, and with a number of copper and tin vessels below it, the wallpaper imitating blue and white tiles, and a couple of colored supplements fluttering from the walls above the kitchen range.

As the dawn grew clearer, we saw through the gap in the wall the body of a Martian, standing sentinel, I suppose, over the still glowing cylinder. At the sight of that we crawled as circumspectly as possible out of the twilight of the kitchen into the darkness of the scullery.

Abruptly the right interpretation dawned upon my mind.

"The fifth cylinder," I whispered, "the fifth shot from Mars, has struck this house and buried us under the ruins!"

For a time the curate was silent, and then he whispered:

"God have mercy upon us!"

I heard him presently whimpering to himself.

Save for that sound we lay quite still in the scullery; I for my part scarce dared breathe, and sat with my eyes fixed on the faint light of the kitchen door. I could just see the curate's face, a dim, oval shape, and his collar and cuffs. Outside there began a metallic hammering, then a violent hooting, and then again, after a quiet interval, a hissing like the hissing of an engine. These noises, for the most part problematical, continued intermittently, and seemed if anything to increase in number as time wore on. Presently a measured thudding and a vibration that made everything about us quiver and the vessels in the pantry ring and shift, began and continued. Once the light was eclipsed, and the ghostly kitchen doorway became absolutely dark. For many hours we must have crouched there, silent and shivering, until our tired attention failed. . . .

At last I found myself awake and very hungry. I am inclined to believe we must have spent the greater portion of a day before that awakening. My hunger was at a stride so insistent that it moved me to action. I told the curate I was going to seek food, and felt my way toward the pantry. He made me no answer, but so soon as I began eating the faint noise I made stirred him up and I heard him crawling after me.

2. What We Saw from the Ruined House

AFTER EATING we crept back to the scullery, and there I must have dozed again, for when presently I looked round I was alone. The thudding vibration continued with wearisome persistence. I whispered for the curate several times, and at last felt my way to the door of the kitchen. It was still daylight, and I perceived him across the room, lying against the triangular hole that looked out upon the Martians. His shoulders were hunched, so that his head was hidden from me.

I could hear a number of noises almost like those in an engine shed; and the place rocked with that beating thud. Through the aperture in the wall I could see the top of a tree touched with gold and the warm blue of a tranquil evening sky. For a minute or so I remained watching the curate, and then I advanced, crouching and stepping with extreme care amid the broken crockery that littered the floor.

I touched the curate's leg, and he started so violently that a mass of plaster went sliding down outside and fell with a loud impact. I gripped his arm, fearing he might cry out, and for a long time we crouched motionless. Then I turned to see how much of our rampart remained. The detachment of the plaster had left a vertical slit open in the débris, and by raising myself cautiously across a beam I was able to see out of this gap into what had been overnight a quiet suburban roadway. Vast, indeed, was the change that we beheld.

The fifth cylinder must have fallen right into the midst of the house we had first visited. The building had vanished, completely smashed, pulverized, and dispersed by the blow. The cylinder lay now far beneath the original foundations — deep in a hole, already vastly larger than the pit I had looked into at Woking. The earth all round it had splashed under that tremendous impact — "splashed" is the only word — and lay in heaped piles that hid the masses of the adjacent houses. It had behaved exactly like mud under the violent blow of a hammer. Our house had collapsed backward; the front portion, even on the ground floor, had been destroyed completely; by a chance the kitchen and scullery had escaped, and stood buried now under soil and ruins, closed in by tons of earth on every side save toward the cylinder. Over that aspect we hung now on the very edge of the great circular pit the Martians were engaged in making. The heavy beating sound was evidently just behind us, and ever and again a bright green vapor drove up like a veil across our peephole.

The cylinder was already opened in the center of the pit, and on the farther edge of the pit, amid the smashed and gravel-heaped shrubbery, one of the great fighting machines, deserted by its occupant, stood stiff and tall against the evening sky. At first I scarcely noticed the pit and the cylinder, although it has been convenient to describe them first, on account of the extraordinary glittering mechanism I saw busy in the excavation, and on account of the strange creatures that were crawling slowly and painfully across the heaped mold near it.

The mechanism it certainly was that held my attention first. It was one of those complicated fabrics that have since been called handling machines, and the study of which has already given such an enormous impetus to terrestrial invention. As it dawned upon me first it presented a sort of metallic spider with five jointed, agile legs, and with an extraordinary number of jointed levers, bars, and reaching and clutching tentacles about its body. Most of its arms were retracted, but with three long tentacles it was fishing out a number of rods, plates, and bars which lined the covering and apparently strengthened the walls, of the cylinder. These, as it extracted them, were lifted out and deposited upon a level surface of earth behind it.

Its motion was so swift, complex, and perfect that at first I did not see it as a machine, in spite of its metallic glitter. The fighting machines were coordinated and animated to an extraordinary pitch, but nothing to compare with this. People who have never seen these structures, and have only the ill-imagined efforts of artists or the imperfect descriptions of such eyewitnesses as myself to go upon, scarcely realize that living quality.

I recall particularly the illustration of one of the first pamphlets to give a consecutive account of the war. The artist had evidently made a hasty study of one of the fighting machines, and there his knowledge ended. He presented them as tilted, stiff tripods, without either flexibility or subtlety, and with an altogether misleading monotony of effect. The pamphlet containing these renderings had a considerable vogue, and I mention them here simply to warn the reader against the impression they may have created. They were no more like the Martians I saw in action than a Dutch doll is like a human being. To my mind, the pamphlet would have been much better without them.

At first, I say, the handling machine did not impress me as a machine, but as a crablike creature with a glittering integument, the controlling Martian whose delicate tentacles actuated its movements seeming to be simply the equivalent of the crab's cerebral portion. But then I perceived the resemblance of its gray-brown, shiny, leathery integument to that of the other sprawling bodies beyond, and the true nature of this dexterous workman dawned upon me. With that realization my interest shifted to those other creatures, the real Martians. Already I had had a transient impression of these, and the first nausea no longer obscured my observation. Moreover, I was concealed and and motionless, and under no urgency of action.

They were, I now saw, the most unearthly creatures it is possible to conceive. They were huge round bodies — or, rather, heads — about four feet in diameter, each body having in front of it a face. This face had no nostrils — indeed, the Martians do not seem to have had any sense of smell, but it had a pair of very large dark-colored eyes, and just beneath this a kind of fleshy beak. In the back of this head or body — I scarcely know how to speak of it — was the single tight tympanic surface, since known to be anatomically an ear, though it must have been almost useless in our denser air. In a group round the mouth were sixteen slender, almost whiplike tentacles, arranged in two bunches of eight each. These bunches have since been named rather aptly, by that distinguished anatomist, Professor Howes, the *hands*. Even as I saw these Martians for the first time they seemed to be endeavoring to raise themselves on these hands, but of course, with the increased weight of terrestrial conditions, this was impossible. There is reason to suppose that on Mars they may have progressed upon them with some facility.

The internal anatomy, I may remark here, as dissection has since shown, was almost equally simple. The greater part of the structure was the brain, sending enormous nerves to the eyes, ear, and tactile tentacles. Besides this were the bulky lungs, into which the mouth opened, and the heart and its vessels. The pulmonary distress caused by the denser atmosphere and greater gravitational attraction was only too evident in the convulsive movements of the outer skin.

And this was the sum of the Martian organs. Strange as it may seem to a human being, all the complex apparatus of digestion, which makes up the bulk of our bodies, did not exist in the Martians. They were heads — merely heads. Entrails they had none. They did not eat, much less digest. Instead, they took the fresh, living blood of other creatures, and *injected* it into their own veins. I have myself seen this being done, as I shall mention in its place. But, squeamish as I may seem, I cannot bring myself to describe what I could not endure even to continue watching. Let it suffice to say, blood obtained from a still living animal, in most cases from a human being, was run directly by means of a little pipette into the recipient canal. . . .

The bare idea of this is no doubt horribly repulsive to us, but at the same time I think that we should remember how repulsive our carnivorous habits would seem to an intelligent rabbit.

The physiological advantages of the practice of injection are undeniable, if one thinks of the tremendous waste of human time and energy occasioned by eating and the digestive process. Our bodies are half made up of glands and tubes and organs, occupied in turning heterogeneous food into blood. The digestive processes and their reaction upon the nervous system sap our strength and color our minds. Men go happy or miserable as they have healthy or unhealthy livers, or sound gastric glands. But the Martians were lifted above all these organic fluctuations of mood and emotion.

Their undeniable preference for men as their source of nourishment is partly explained by the nature of the remains of the victims they

had brought with them as provisions from
Mars. These creatures, to judge from the shriveled remains that have fallen into human
hands, were bipeds with flimsy, silicious skeletons (almost like those of the silicious sponges)
and feeble musculature, standing about six feet
high and having round, erect heads, and large
eyes in flinty sockets. Two or three of these
seem to have been brought in each cylinder,
and all were killed before earth was reached. It
was just as well for them, for the mere attempt
to stand upright upon our planet would have
broken every bone in their bodies.

And while I am engaged in this description,
I may add in this place certain further details
which, although they were not all evident to us
at the time, will enable the reader who is unac-
quainted with them to form a clearer picture of
these offensive creatures.

In three other points their physiology differed strangely from ours. Their organisms did
not sleep, any more than the heart of man
sleeps. Since they had no extensive muscular
mechanism to recuperate, that periodical extinction was unknown to them. They had little
or no sense of fatigue, it would seem. On earth
they could never have moved without effort, yet
even to the last they kept in action. In twenty-
four hours they did twenty-four hours of work,
as even on earth is perhaps the case with the
ants.

In the next place, wonderful as it seems in a sexual world, the Martians were absolutely without sex, and therefore without any of the tumultuous emotions that arise from that difference among men. A young Martian, there can now be no dispute, was really born upon earth during the war, and it was found attached to its parent, partially *budded* off, just as young lily bulbs bud off, or like the young animals in the fresh-water polyp.

In man, in all the higher terrestrial animals, such a method of increase has disappeared; but even on this earth it was certainly the primitive method. Among the lower animals, up even to those first cousins of the vertebrated animals, the Tunicates, the two processes occur side by side, but finally the sexual method superseded its competitor altogether. On Mars, however, just the reverse has apparently been the case.

It is worthy of remark that a certain speculative writer of quasi-scientific repute, writing long before the Martian invasion, did forecast for man a final structure not unlike the actual Martian condition. His prophecy, I remember, appeared in November or December, 1893, in a long defunct publication, the *Pall Mall Budget*, and I recall a caricature of it in a pre-Martian periodical called *Punch*. He pointed out — writing in a foolish, facetious tone — that the perfection of mechanical appliances must ulti-

mately supersede limbs; the perfection of
chemical devices, digestion; that such organs
as hair, external nose, teeth, ears, and chin were
no longer essential parts of the human being,
and that the tendency of natural selection
would lie in the direction of their steady dimi-
nution through the coming ages. The brain
alone remained a cardinal necessity. Only one
other part of the body had a strong case for
survival, and that was the hand, "teacher and
agent of the brain." While the rest of the body
dwindled, the hands would grow larger.

There is many a true word written in jest,
and here in the Martians we have beyond dispute the actual accomplishment of such a sup-
pression of the animal side of the organism by
the intelligence. To me it is quite credible that
the Martians may be descended from beings not
unlike ourselves, by a gradual development of
brain and hands (the latter giving rise to the
two bunches of delicate tentacles at last) at
the expense of the rest of the body. Without the
body the brain would, of course, become a mere
selfish intelligence, without any of the emotional substratum of the human being.

The last salient point in which the systems of
these creatures differed from ours was in what
one might have thought a very trivial particular. Microorganisms, which cause so much
disease and pain on earth, have either never appeared upon Mars or Martian sanitary science

eliminated them ages ago. A hundred diseases, all the fevers and contagions of human life, consumption, cancers, tumors and such morbidities, never enter the scheme of their life. And speaking of the differences between the life on Mars and terrestrial life, I may allude here to the curious suggestions of the red weed.

Apparently the vegetable kingdom in Mars, instead of having green for a dominant color, is of a vivid blood-red tint. At any rate, the seeds which the Martians (intentionally or accidentally) brought with them gave rise in all cases to red-colored growths. Only that known popularly as the red weed, however, gained any footing in competition with terrestrial forms. The red creeper was quite a transitory growth, and few people have seen it growing. For a time, however, the red weed grew with astonishing vigor and luxuriance. It spread up the sides of the pit by the third or fourth day of our imprisonment, and its cactuslike branches formed a carmine fringe to the edges of our triangular window. And afterward I found it broadcast throughout the country, and especially wherever there was a stream of water.

The Martians had what appears to have been an auditory organ, a single round drum at the back of the head-body, and eyes with a visual range not very different from ours except that, according to Philips, blue and violet were as black to them. It is commonly supposed that

they communicated by sounds and tentacular
gesticulations; this is asserted, for instance, in
the able but hastily compiled pamphlet (written
evidently by someone not an eyewitness of Martian actions) to which I have already alluded,
and which, so far, has been the chief source of
information concerning them. Now no surviv-
ing human being saw so much of the Martians
in action as I did. I take no credit to myself for
an accident, but the fact is so. And I assert that
I watched them closely time after time, and
that I have seen four, five, and (once) six of
them sluggishly performing the most elabor-
ately complicated operations together without
either sound or gesture. Their peculiar hooting
invariably preceeded feeding; it had no modu-
lation, and was, I believe, in no sense a signal,
but merely the expiration of air preparatory to
the suctional operation. I have a certain claim
to at least an elementary knowledge of psychol-
ogy, and in this matter I am convinced — as
firmly as I am convinced of anything — that
the Martians interchanged thoughts without
any physical intermediation. And I have been
convinced of this in spite of strong preconcep-
tions. Before the Martian invasion, as an occasional reader here or there may remember, I
had written with some little vehemence against
the telepathic theory.

The Martians wore no clothing. Their con-
ceptions of ornament and decorum were neces-

sarily different from ours; and not only were
they evidently much less sensible of changes of
temperature than we are, but changes of pressure do not seem to have affected their health at
all seriously. Yet though they wore no clothing,
it was in the other artificial additions to their
bodily resources that their great superiority
over man lay. We men, with our bicycles and
road skates, our Lilienthal soaring machines,
our guns and sticks and so forth, are just in
the beginning of the evolution that the Martians have worked out. They have become practically mere brains, wearing different bodies
according to their needs just as men wear suits
of clothes and take a bicycle in a hurry or an
umbrella in the wet. And of their appliances,
perhaps nothing is more wonderful to a man
than the curious fact that what is the dominant
feature of almost all human devices in mechanism is absent — the *wheel* is absent; among all
the things they brought to earth there is no
trace or suggestion of their use of wheels. One
would have at least expected it in locomotion.
And in this connection it is curious to remark
that even on this earth nature has never hit
upon the wheel, or has preferred other expedi-
ents to its development. And not only did the
Martians either not know of (which is incredible), or abstain from, the wheel, but in their
apparatus singularly little use is made of the
fixed pivot, or relatively fixed pivot, with circu-

lar motions thereabout confined to one plane.
Almost all the joints of the machinery present
a complicated system of sliding parts moving
over small but beautifully curved friction bear-
ings. And while upon this matter of detail, it is
remarkable that the long leverages of their machines are in most cases actuated by a sort of
sham musculature of disks in an elastic sheath;
these disks become polarized and drawn closely
and powerfully together when traversed by a
current of electricity. In this way the curious
parallelism to animal motions, which was so
striking and disturbing to the human beholder,
was attained. Such quasi-muscles abounded in
the crablike handling machine which, on my
first peeping out of the slit, I watched unpack-
ing the cylinder. It seemed infinitely more alive
than the actual Martians lying beyond it in the
sunset light, panting, stirring ineffectual tentacles, and moving feebly after their vast journey
across space.

While I was still watching their sluggish motions in the sunlight, and noting each strange
detail of their form, the curate reminded me of
his presence by pulling violently at my arm. I
turned to a scowling face, and silent, eloquent
lips. He wanted the slit, which permitted only
one of us to peep through; and so I had to forgo
watching them for a time while he enjoyed that
privilege.

When I looked again, the busy handling machine had already put together several of the pieces of apparatus it had taken out of the cylinder into a shape having an unmistakable likeness to its own; and down on the left a busy little digging mechanism had come into view, emitting jets of green vapor and working its way round the pit, excavating and embanking in a methodical and discriminating manner. This it was which had caused the regular beating noise, and the rhythmic shocks that had kept our ruinous refuge quivering. It piped and whistled as it worked. So far as I could see, the thing was without a directing Martian at all.

3. The Days of Imprisonment

THE ARRIVAL of a second fighting machine drove us from our peephole into the scullery, for we feared that from his elevation the Martian might see down upon us behind our barrier. At a later date we began to feel less in danger of their eyes, for to an eye in the dazzle of the sunlight outside our refuge must have been blank blackness, but at first the slightest suggestion of approach drove us into the scullery in heart-throbbing retreat. Yet terrible as was the danger we incurred, the attraction of peeping was for both of us irresistible. And I recall now with a sort of wonder that, in spite of the infinite danger in which we were between starvation and a still more terrible death, we could yet struggle bitterly for that horrible privilege of sight. We would race across the kitchen in a grotesque way between eagerness and the dread of making a noise, and strike each other, and thrust and kick, within a few inches of exposure.

The fact is that we had absolutely incompatible dispositions and habits of thought and action, and our danger and isolation only accentuated the incompatibility. At Halliford I had already come to hate the curate's trick of helpless exclamation, his stupid rigidity of mind. His endless muttering monologue vitiated every effort I made to think out a line of action, and drove me at times, thus pent up and intensified, almost to the verge of craziness. He was as lacking in restraint as a silly woman. He would weep for hours together, and I verily believe that to the very end this spoiled child of life thought his weak tears in some way efficacious. And I would sit in the darkness unable to keep my mind off him by reason of his importunities. He ate more than I did, and it was in vain I pointed out that our only chance of life was to stop in the house until the Martians had done with their pit, that in that long patience a time might presently come when we should need food. He ate and drank impulsively in heavy meals at long intervals. He slept little.

As the days wore on, his utter carelessness of any consideration so intensified our distress and danger that I had, much as I loathed doing it, to resort to threats, and at last to blows. That brought him to reason for a time. But he was one of those weak creatures, void of pride, timorous, anemic, hateful souls, full of shifty cunning who face neither God nor man, who face not even themselves.

It is disagreeable for me to recall and write these things, but I set them down that my story may lack nothing. Those who have escaped the dark and terrible aspects of life will find my brutality, my flash of rage in our final tragedy, easy enough to blame; for they know what is wrong as well as any, but not what is possible to tortured men. But those who have been under the shadow, who have gone down at last to elemental things, will have a wider charity.

And while within we fought out our dark, dim contest of whispers, snatched food and drink, and gripping hands and blows, without, in the pitiless sunlight of that terrible June, was the strange wonder, the unfamiliar routine of the Martians in the pit. Let me return to those first new experiences of mine. After a long time I ventured back to the peephole, to find that the newcomers had been reinforced by the occupants of no fewer than three of the fighting machines. These last had brought with them certain fresh appliances that stood in an orderly manner

about the cylinder. The second handling machine was now completed, and was busied in
serving one of the novel contrivances the big
machine had brought. This was a body resembling a milk can in its general form, above
which oscillated a pear-shaped receptacle, and
from which a stream of white powder flowed
into a circular basin below.

The oscillatory motion was imparted to this
by one tentacle of the handling machine. With
two spatulate hands the handling machine was
digging out and flinging masses of clay into the
pear-shaped receptacle above, while with another arm it periodically opened a door and removed rusty and blackened clinkers from the
middle part of the machine. Another steely
tentacle directed the powder from the basin
along a ribbed channel toward some receiver
that was hidden from me by the mound of bluish dust. From this unseen receiver a little
thread of green smoke rose vertically into the
quiet air. As I looked, the handling machine,
with a faint and musical clinking, extended,
telescopic fashion, a tentacle that had been a
moment before a mere blunt projection, until
its end was hidden behind the mound of clay. In
another second it had lifted a bar of white aluminum into sight, untarnished as yet and shining dazzlingly, and deposited it in a growing
stack of bars that stood at the side of the pit.

Between sunset and starlight this dexterous machine must have made more than a hundred such bars out of the crude clay, and the mound of bluish dust rose steadily until it topped the side of the pit.

The contrast between the swift and complex movements of these contrivances and the inert, panting clumsiness of their masters was acute, and for days I had to tell myself repeatedly that these latter were indeed the living of the two things.

The curate had possession of the slit when the first men were brought to the pit. I was sitting below, huddled up, listening with all my ears. He made a sudden movement backward, and I, fearful that we were observed, crouched in a spasm of terror. He came sliding down the rubbish and crept beside me in the darkness, inarticulate, gesticulating, and for a moment I shared his panic. His gesture suggested a resignation of the slit, and after a little while my curiosity gave me courage, and I rose up, stepped across him, and clambered up to it. At first I could see no reason for his frantic behavior. The twilight had now come, the stars were little and faint, but the pit was illuminated by the flickering green fire that came from the aluminium-making. The whole picture was a flickering scheme of green gleams and shifting rusty black shadows, strangely trying to the eyes. Over and through it all went the bats, heeding it not at all. The sprawling Martians were no longer to be seen, the mound of blue-green powder had risen to cover them from sight, and a fighting machine, with its legs contracted, crumpled, and abbreviated, stood across the corner of the pit. And then, amid the clangor of the machinery, came a drifting suspicion of human voices, that I entertained at first only to dismiss.

I crouched, watching this fighting machine closely, satisfying myself now for the first time that the hood did indeed contain a Martain. As the green flames lifted I could see the oily gleam of his integument and the brightness of his eyes. And suddenly I heard a yell, and saw a long tentacle reaching over the shoulder of the machine to the little cage that hunched upon its back. Then something — something struggling violently — was lifted high against the sky, a black, vague enigma against the starlight; and as this black object came down again, I saw by the green brightness that it was a man. For an instant he was clearly visible. He was a stout, ruddy, middle-aged man, well dressed; three days before he must have been walking the world, a man of considerable consequence. I could see his staring eyes and gleams of light on his studs and watch chain. He vanished behind the mound, and for a moment there was silence.

And then began a shrieking and a sustained
and cheerful hooting from the Martians.

I slid down the rubbish, struggled to my feet,
clapped my hands over my ears, and bolted into
the scullery. The curate, who had been crouching silently with his arms over his head, looked
up as I passed, cried out quite loudly at my
desertion of him, and came running after me.

That night, as we lurked in the scullery bal-
anced between our horror and the terrible fascination this peeping had, although I felt an
urgent need of action I tried in vain to conceive
some plan of escape; but afterward, during the
second day, I was able to consider our position
with great clearness. The curate, I found, was
quite incapable of discussion; this new and cul-
minating atrocity had robbed him of all vestiges of reason or forethought. Practically he
had already sunk to the level of an animal. But,
as the saying goes, I gripped myself with both
hands. It grew upon my mind, once I could face
the facts, that, terrible as our position was,
there was as yet no justification for absolute
despair. Our chief chance lay in the possibility
of the Martians making the pit nothing more
than a temporary encampment. Or even if they
kept it permanently, they might not consider
it necessary to guard it, and a chance of escape
might be afforded us. I also weighed very care-
fully the possibility of our digging a way out in

a direction away from the pit, but the chances of our emerging within sight of some sentinel fighting machine seemed at first too great. And I should have had to do all the digging myself. The curate would certainly have failed me.

It was on the third day, if my memory serves me right, that I saw the lad killed. It was the only occasion on which I actually saw the Martians feed. After that experience I avoided the hole in the wall for the better part of a day. I went into the scullery, removed the door, and spent some hours digging with my hatchet as silently as possible; but when I had made a hole about a couple of feet deep the loose earth collapsed noisily, and I did not dare continue. I lost heart, and lay down on the scullery floor for a long time, having no spirit even to move. And after that I abandoned altogether the idea of escaping by excavation.

It says much for the impression the Martians had made upon me that at first I entertained little or no hope of our escape being brought about by their overthrow through any human effort. But on the fourth or fifth night I heard a sound like heavy guns.

It was very late in the night, and the moon was shining brightly. The Martians had taken away the excavating machine, and, save for a fighting machine that stood in the remoter bank of the pit and a handling machine that was buried out of my sight in a corner of the pit immediately beneath my peephole, the place was deserted by them. Except for the pale glow from the handling machine and the bars and patches of white moonlight, the pit was in darkness, and, except for the clinking of the handling machine, quite still. That night was a beautiful serenity; save for one planet, the moon seemed to have the sky to herself. I heard a dog howling, and that familiar sound it was that made me listen. Then I heard quite distinctly a booming exactly like the sound of great guns. Six distinct reports I counted, and after a long interval six again. And that was all.

4. The Death of the Curate

IT WAS ON THE SIXTH DAY of our imprisonment that I peeped for the last time, and presently found myself alone. Instead of keeping close to me and trying to oust me from the slit, the curate had gone back into the scullery. I was struck by a sudden thought. I went back quickly and quietly into the scullery. In the darkness I heard the curate drinking. I snatched in the darkness, and my fingers caught a bottle of burgundy.

For a few minutes there was a tussle. The bottle struck the floor and broke, and I desisted and rose. We stood panting and threatening each other. In the end I planted myself between him and the food, and told him of my determination to begin a discipline. I divided the food

in the pantry into rations to last us ten days. I
would not let him eat any more that day. In the
afternoon he made a feeble effort to get at the
food. I had been dozing, but in an instant I was
awake. All day and all night we sat face to face,
I weary but resolute, and he weeping and complaining of his immediate hunger. It was, I
know, a night and a day, but to me it seemed —
it seems now — an interminable length of time.

And so our widened incompatibility ended at
last in open conflict. For two vast days we struggled in undertones and wrestling contests.
There were times when I beat and kicked him
madly, times when I cajoled and persuaded him,
and once I tried to bribe him with the last bottle of burgundy, for there was a rain-water
pump from which I could get water. But neither
force nor kindness availed; he was indeed beyond reason. He would neither desist from his
attacks on the food nor from his noisy babbling
to himself. The rudimentary precautions to
keep our imprisonment endurable he would not
observe. Slowly I began to realize the complete
overthrow of his intelligence, to perceive that
my sole companion in this close and sickly darkness was a man insane.

From certain vague memories I am inclined
to think my own mind wandered at times. I had
strange and hideous dreams whenever I slept.
It sounds paradoxical, but I am inclined to

think that the weakness and insanity of the curate warned me, braced me, and kept me a sane man.

On the eighth day he began to talk aloud instead of whispering, and nothing I could do would moderate his speech.

"It is just, O God!" he would say, over and over again. "It is just. On me and mine be the punishment laid. We have sinned, we have fallen short. There was poverty, sorrow; the poor were trodden in the dust, and I held my peace. I preached acceptable folly — my God, what folly! — when I should have stood up, though I died for it, and called upon them to repent — repent! . . . Oppressors of the poor and needy! . . . The winepress of God!"

Then he would suddenly revert to the matter of the food I withheld from him, praying, begging, weeping, at last threatening. He began to raise his voice — I prayed him not to. He perceived a hold on me — he threatened he would shout and bring the Martians upon us. For a time that scared me; but any concession would have shortened our chance of escape beyond estimating. I defied him, although I felt no assurance that he might not do this thing. But that day, at any rate, he did not. He talked with his voice rising slowly, through the greater part of the eighth and ninth days — threats, entreaties, mingled with a torrent of half-sane

and always frothy repentance for his vacant
sham of God's service, such as made me pity
him. Then he slept awhile, and began again with
renewed strength, so loudly that I must needs
make him desist.

"Be still!" I implored.

He rose to his knees, for he had been sitting
in the darkness near the copper.

"I have been still too long," he said, in a tone
that must have reached the pit, "and now I
must bear my witness. Woe unto this unfaith-
ful city! Woe! Woe! Woe! Woe! Woe to the inhabitants of the earth by reason of the other
voices of the trumpet——"

"Shut up" I said, rising to my feet, and in a
terror lest the Martians should hear us. "For
God's sake——"

"Nay," shouted the curate, at the top of his
voice, standing likewise and extending his
arms. "Speak! The word of the Lord is upon
me!"

In three strides he was at the door leading
into the kitchen. "I must bear my witness! I go!
It has already been too long delayed."

I put out my hand and felt the meat chopper
hanging to the wall. In a flash I was after him.
I was fierce with fear. Before he was halfway
across the kitchen I had overtaken him. With
one last touch of humanity I turned the blade
back and struck him with the butt. He went

headlong forward and lay stretched on the ground. I stumbled over him and stood panting. He lay still.

Suddenly I heard a noise without, the run and smash of slipping plaster, and the triangular aperture in the wall was darkened. I looked up and saw the lower surface of the handling machine coming slowly across the hole. One of its gripping limbs curled amid the débris; another limb appeared, feeling its way over the fallen beams. I stood petrified, staring. Then I saw through a sort of glass plate near the edge of the body the face, as we may call it, and the large dark eyes of a Martian, peering, and then a long metallic snake of tentacle came feeling slowly through the hole.

I turned by an effort, stumbled over the curate, and stopped at the scullery door. The tentacle was now some way, two yards or more, in the room, and twisting and turning, with queer sudden movements, this way and that. For a while I stood fascinated by that slow, fitful advance. Then, with a faint, hoarse cry, I forced myself across the scullery, I trembled violently; I could scarcely stand upright. I opened the door of the coal cellar, and stood there in the darkness staring at the faintly lit doorway into the kitchen, and listening. Had the Martian seen me? What was it doing now?

Something was moving to and fro there,

very quietly; every now and then it tapped
against the wall, or started on its movements
with a faint metallic ringing, like the movements of keys on a split-ring. Then a heavy
body — I knew too well what — was dragged
across the floor of the kitchen toward the
opening. Irresistibly attracted, I crept to the
door and peeped into the kitchen. In the triangle of bright outer sunlight I saw the Martian, in its Briareus of a handling machine,
scrutinizing the curate's head. I thought at
once that it would infer my presence from the
mark of the blow I had given him.

I crept back to the coal cellar, shut the door,
and began to cover myself up as much as I
could, and as noiselessly as possible in the
darkness, among the firewood and coal therein.
Every now and then I paused, rigid, to hear if
the Martian had thrust its tentacle through
the opening again.

Then the faint metallic jingle returned. I
traced it slowly feeling over the kitchen. Presently I heard it nearer — in the scullery, as
I judged. I thought that its length might be
insufficient to reach me. I prayed copiously. It
passed, scraping faintly across the cellar door.
An age of almost intolerable suspense intervened; then I heard it fumbling at the latch!
It had found the door! The Martians understood doors!

It worried at the catch for a minute, perhaps, and then the door opened.

In the darkness I could just see the thing — like an elephant's trunk more than anything else — waving toward me and touching and examining the wall, coals, wood, and ceiling. It was like a black worm swaying its blind head to and fro.

Once, even, it touched the heel of my boot. I was on the verge of screaming; I bit my hand. For a time the tentacle was silent. I could have fancied it had been withdrawn. Presently, with an abrupt click, it gripped something — I thought it had me! — and seemed to go out of the cellar again. For a minute I was not sure. Apparently it had taken a lump of coal to examine.

I seized the opportunity of slightly shifting my position, which had become cramped, and then listened. I whispered passionate prayers for safety.

Then I heard the slow, deliberate sound creeping toward me again. Slowly, slowly it drew near, scratching against the walls and tapping the furniture.

While I was still doubtful, it rapped smartly against the cellar door and closed it. I heard it go into the pantry, and the biscuit tins rattled and a bottle smashed, and then came a heavy bump against the cellar door. Then silence, that passed into an infinity of suspense.

Had it gone?

At last I decided that it had.

It came into the scullery no more; but I lay all the tenth day in the close darkness, buried among coals and firewood, not daring even to crawl out for the drink for which I craved. It was the eleventh day before I ventured so far from my security.

5. The Stillness

MY FIRST ACT before I went into the pantry was to fasten the door between the kitchen and the scullery. But the pantry was empty; every scrap of food had gone. Apparently, the Martian had taken it all on the previous day. At that discovery I despaired for the first time. I took no food, or no drink either, on the eleventh or the twelfth day.

At first my mouth and throat were parched, and my strength ebbed sensibly. I sat about in the darkness of the scullery, in a state of despondent wretchedness. My mind ran on eating. I thought I had become deaf, for the noises of movement I had been accustomed to hear from the pit had ceased absolutely. I did not feel strong enough to crawl noiselessly to the peephole, or I would have gone there.

On the twelfth day my throat was so painful that, taking the chance of alarming the Martians, I attacked the creaking rain-water pump that stood by the sink, and got a couple of glassfuls of blackened and tainted rain water. I was greatly refreshed by this, and emboldened by the fact that no inquiring tentacle followed the noise of my pumping.

During these days, in a rambling, inconclusive way, I thought much of the curate and of the manner of his death.

On the thirteenth day I drank some more water, and dozed and thought disjointedly of eating and of vague impossible plans of escape. Whenever I dozed I dreamed of horrible phantasms, of the death of the curate, or of sumptuous dinners; but, asleep or awake, I felt a keen pain that urged me to drink again and again. The light that came into the scullery was no longer gray, but red. To my disordered imagination it seemed the color of blood.

On the fourteenth day I went into the kitchen, and I was surprised to find that the fronds of the red weed had grown right across the hole in the wall, turning the half-light of the place into a crimson-colored obscurity.

It was early on the fifteenth day that I heard a curious, familiar sequence of sounds in the kitchen, and, listening, identified it as the

snuffing and scratching of a dog. Going into
the kitchen, I saw a dog's nose peering in
through a break among the ruddy fronds. This
greatly surprised me. At the scent of me he
barked shortly.

I thought if I could induce him to come
into the place quietly I should be able, perhaps,
to kill and eat him; and in any case, it would
be advisable to kill him, lest his actions attracted the attention of the Martians.

I crept forward, saying, "Good dog!" very
softly; but he suddenly withdrew his head and
disappeared.

I listened — I was not deaf — but certainly
the pit was still. I heard a sound like the flutter
of a bird's wings, and a hoarse croaking, but
that was all.

For a long while I lay close to the peephole,
but not daring to move aside the red plants
that obscured it. Once or twice I heard a faint
pitter-patter like the feet of the dog going
hither and thither on the sand far below me,
and there were more birdlike sounds, but that
was all. At length, encouraged by the silence,
I looked out.

Except in the corner, where a multitude of
crows hopped and fought over the skeletons
of the dead the Martians had consumed, there
was not a living thing in the pit.

I stared about me, scarcely believing my
eyes. All the machinery had gone. Save for the

big mound of grayish-blue powder in one corner, certain bars of aluminum in another, the
black birds, and the skeletons of the killed,
the place was merely an empty circular pit in
the sand.

Slowly I thrust myself out through the red
weed, and stood upon the mound of rubble. I
could see in any direction save behind me, to
the north, and neither Martians nor sign of
Martians were to be seen. The pit dropped
sheerly from my feet, but a little way along
the rubbish afforded a practicable slope to
the summit of the ruins. My chance of escape
had come. I began to tremble.

I hesitated for some time, and then, in a
gust of desperate resolution, and with a heart
that throbbed violently, I scrambled to the top
of the mound in which I had been buried so
long.

I looked about again. To the northward,
too, no Martian was visible.

When I had last seen this part of Sheen in
the daylight it had been a straggling street of
comfortable white and red houses, inter-
spersed with abundant shady trees. Now I
stood on a mound of smashed brickwork, clay,
and gravel, over which spread a multitude of
red cactus-shaped plants, knee-high, without a
solitary terrestrial growth to dispute their
footing. The trees near me were dead and

brown, but further a netword of red threads
scaled the still living stems.

The neighboring houses had all been wrecked,
but none had been burned; their walls stood,
sometimes to the second story, with smashed
windows and shattered doors. The red weed
grew tumultuously in their roofless rooms.
Below me was the great pit, with the crows
struggling for its refuse. A number of other
birds hopped about among the ruins. Far away
I saw a gaunt cat slink crouchingly among a
wall, but traces of men there were none.

The day seemed, by contrast with my recent confinement, dazzlingly bright, the sky a
glowing blue. A gentle breeze kept the red
weed that covered every scrap of unoccupied
ground gently swaying. And oh! the sweetness
of the air!

6. The Work of Fifteen Days

FOR SOME TIME I stood tottering on the mound regardless of my safety. Within that noisome den from which I had emerged I had thought with a narrow intensity only of our immediate security. I had not realized what had been happening to the world, had not anticipated this startling vision of unfamiliar things. I had expected to see Sheen in ruins — I found about me the landscape, weird and lurid, of another planet.

For that moment I touched an emotion beyond the common range of men, yet one that the poor brutes we dominate know only too well. I felt as a rabbit might feel returning to his burrow and suddenly confronted by the work of a dozen busy navvies, digging the foundations of a house. I felt the first inkling of a thing that presently grew quite clear in my mind, that oppressed me for many days, a sense of dethronement, a persuasion that I was no longer a master, but an animal among the animals, under the Martian heel. With us it would be as with them, to lurk and watch, to run and hide; the fear and empire of man had passed away.

But so soon as this strangeness had been realized it passed, and my dominant motive became the hunger of my long and dismal fast. In the direction away from the pit I saw, beyond a red-covered wall, a patch of garden ground unburied. This gave me a hint, and I went knee-deep, and sometimes neck-deep, in the red weed. The density of the weed gave me a reassuring sense of hiding. The wall was some six feet high, and when I attempted to clamber it I found I could not lift my feet to the crest. So I went along by the side of it, and came to a corner and a rockwork that enabled me to get to the top, and tumble into the garden I coveted. Here I found some young onions, a couple of gladiolus bulbs, and a quantity of immature carrots, all of which I secured, and, scrambling over a ruined wall, went on my way through scarlet and crimson trees toward Kew — it was like walking through an avenue of gigantic blood drops — possessed with two ideas: to get more food, and to limp, as soon and as far as my strength permitted, out of this accursed unearthly region of the pit.

Some way farther, in a grassy place, was a group of mushrooms which also I devoured, and then I came upon a brown sheet of flowing shallow water, where meadows used to be. These fragments of nourishment served only to whet my hunger. At first I was surprised at this flood in a hot, dry summer, but afterward I discovered that it was caused by the tropical exuberance of the red weed. Directly this extraordinary growth encountered water it straightway became gigantic and of unparalleled fecundity. Its seeds were simply poured down into the water of the Wey and Thames, and its swiftly growing and Titanic water-fronds speedily choked both those rivers.

At Putney, as I afterward saw, the bridge was almost lost in a tangle of this weed, and at Richmond, too, the Thames water poured in a broad and shallow stream across the meadows of Hampton and Twickenham. As the waters spread the weed followed them, until the ruined villas of the Thames valley were for a time lost in this red swamp, whose margin I explored and much of the desolation the Martians had caused was concealed.

In the end the red weed succumbed almost as quickly as it had spread. A cankering disease, due, it is believed, to the action of certain bacteria, presently seized upon it. Now by the action of natural selection, all terrestrial plants have acquired a resisting power against bacterial diseases — they never succumb without a severe struggle, but the red weed rotted like a thing already dead. The fronds became bleached, and then shriveled and brittle. They broke off at the least touch, and the waters that had stimulated their early growth carried their last vestiges out to sea.

My first act on coming to this water was, of course, to slake my thirst. I drank a great deal of it and, moved by an impulse, gnawed some fronds of red weed; but they were watery, and had a sickly, metallic taste. I found the water was sufficiently shallow for me to wade securely, although the red weed impeded my feet a little; but the flood evidently got deeper toward the river, and I turned back to Mortlake. I managed to make out the road by means of occasional ruins of its villas and fences and lamps, and so presently I got out of this spate and made my way to the hill going up toward Roehampton and came out on Putney Common.

Here the scenery changed from the strange and unfamiliar to the wreckage of the familiar: patches of ground exhibited the devastation of a cyclone, and in a few score yards I would come upon perfectly undisturbed spaces, houses with their blinds trimly drawn and doors

closed, as if they had been left for a day by
the owners, or as if their inhabitants slept
within. The red weed was less abundant; the
tall trees along the lane were free from the red
creeper. I hunted for food among the trees,
finding nothing, and I also raided a couple of
silent houses, but they had already been broken
into and ransacked. I rested for the remainder
of the daylight in a shrubbery, being, in my
enfeebled condition, too fatigued to push on.

All this time I saw no human beings, and
no signs of the Martians. I encountered a couple of hungry-looking dogs, but both hurried
circuitously away from the advances I made
them. Near Roehampton I had seen two human skeletons — not bodies, but skeletons,
picked clean — and in the wood by me I found
the crushed and scattered bones of several
cats and rabbits and the skull of a sheep. But
though I gnawed parts of these in my mouth,
there was nothing to be got from them.

After sunset I struggled on along the road
toward Putney, where I think the Heat Ray
must have been used for some reason. And in
a garden beyond Roehampton I got a quantity
of immature potatoes, sufficient to stay my
hunger. From this garden one looked down
upon Putney and the river. The aspect of the
place in the dusk was singularly desolate:
blackened trees, blackened, desolate ruins,
and down the hill the sheets of the flooded

river, red-tinged with the weed. And over all —
silence. It filled me with indescribable terror
to think how swiftly that desolating change
had come.

For a time I believed that mankind had been
swept out of existence, and that I stood there
alone, the last man left alive. Hard by the top
of Putney Hill I came upon another skeleton,
with the arms dislocated and removed several
yards from the rest of the body. As I proceeded I became more and more convinced
that the extermination of mankind was, save
for such stragglers as myself, already accom-
plished in this part of the world. The Martians,
I thought, had gone on and left the country
desolated, seeking food elsewhere. Perhaps even
now they were destroying Berlin or Paris, or it
might be they had gone northward.

7. The Man on Putney Hill

I SPENT THAT NIGHT in the inn that stands at the top of Putney Hill, sleeping in a made bed for the first time since my flight to Leatherhead. I will not tell the needless trouble I had breaking into that house — afterward I found the front door was on the latch — nor how I ransacked every room for food, until, just on the verge of despair, in what seemed to me to be a servant's bedroom, I found a rat-gnawed crust and two tins of pineapple. The place had been already searched and emptied. In the bar I afterward found some biscuits and sandwiches that had been overlooked. The latter I could not eat, they were too rotten, but the former not only stayed my hunger, but filled my pockets. I lit no lamps, fearing some Mar-

232

tian might come beating that part of London
for food in the night. Before I went to bed I
had an interval of restlessness, and prowled
from window to window, peering out for some
sign of these monsters. I slept little. As I lay
in bed I found myself thinking consecutively —
a thing I do not remember to have done since
my last argument with the curate. During all
the intervening time my mental condition had
been a hurrying succession of vague emotional
states or a sort of stupid receptivity. But in
the night my brain, reinforced, I suppose, by
the food I had eaten, grew clear again, and I
thought.

Three things struggled for possession of my
mind: the killing of the curate, the where-
abouts of the Martians, and the possible fate
of my wife. The former gave me no sensation
of horror or remorse to recall; I saw it simply
as a thing done, a memory infinitely disagreeable but quite without the quality of remorse.
I saw myself then as I see myself now, driven
step by step toward that hasty blow, the creature of a sequence of accidents leading inevitably to that. I felt no condemnation; yet the
memory, static, unprogressive, haunted me. In
the silence of the night, with that sense of
the nearness of God that sometimes comes into
the stillness and the darkness, I stood my trial,
my only trial, for that moment of wrath and
fear. I retraced every step of our conversation

from the moment when I had found him
crouching beside me, heedless of my thirst, and
pointing to the fire and smoke that streamed
up from the ruins of Weybridge. We had been
incapable of cooperation — grim chance had
taken no heed of that. Had I foreseen, I should
have left him at Halliford. But I did not foresee; and crime is to foresee and do. And I set
this down as I have set all this story down, as
it was. There were no witnesses — all these
things I might have concealed. But I set it
down, and the reader must form his judgment
as he will.

And when, by an effort, I had set aside that
picture of a prostrate body, I faced the problem of the Martians and the fate of my wife.
For the former I had no data; I could imagine
a hundred things, and so, unhappily, I could
for the latter. And suddenly that night became terrible. I found myself sitting up in bed,
staring at the dark. I found myself praying
that the Heat Ray might have suddenly and
painlessly struck her out of being. Since the
night of my return from Leatherhead I had
not prayed. I had uttered prayers, fetish
prayers, had prayed as heathens mutter
charms when I was in extremity; but now I
prayed indeed, pleading steadfastly and sanely,
face to face with the darkness of God. Strange
night! strangest in this, that so soon as dawn
had come, I, who had talked with God, crept

out of the house like a rat leaving its hiding place — a creature scarcely larger, an inferior animal, a thing that for any passing whim of our masters might be hunted and killed. Perhaps they also prayed confidently to God. Surely, if we have learned nothing else, this war has taught us pity — pity for those witless souls that suffer our dominion.

The morning was bright and fine, and the eastern sky glowed pink, and was fretted with little golden clouds. In the road that runs from the top of Putney Hill to Wimbledon was a number of poor vestiges of the panic torrent that must have poured Londonward on the Sunday night after the fighting began. There was a little two-wheeled cart inscribed with the name of Thomas Lobb, Greengrocer, New Malden, with a smashed wheel and an abandoned tin trunk; there was a straw hat trampled into the now hardened mud, and at the top of West Hill a lot of bloodstained glass about the overturned water trough. My movements were languid, my plans of the vaguest. I had an idea of going to Leatherhead, though I knew that there I had the poorest chance of finding my wife. Certainly, unless death had overtaken them suddenly, my cousins and she would have fled thence; but it seemed to me I might find or learn there whither the Surrey people had fled. I knew I wanted to find my wife, that my heart ached for her and the world of men, but I had no clear idea how the finding might be done. I was also sharply aware now of my intense loneliness. From the corner I went, under cover of a thicket of trees and bushes, to the edge of Wimbledon Common, stretching wide and far.

That dark expanse was lit in patches by yellow gorse and broom; there was no red weed to be seen, and as I prowled, hesitating, on the verge of the open, the sun rose, flooding it all with light and vitality. I came upon a busy swarm of little frogs in a swampy place among the trees. I stopped to look at them, drawing a lesson from their stout resolve to live. And presently, turning suddenly, with an odd feeling of being watched, I beheld something crouching amid a clump of bushes. I stood regarding this. I made a step toward it, and it rose up and became a man armed with a cutlass. I approached him slowly. He stood silent and motionless, regarding me.

As I drew nearer I perceived he was dressed in clothes as dusty and filthy as my own; he looked, indeed, as though he had been dragged through a culvert. Nearer, I distinguished the green slime of ditches mixing with the pale drab of dried clay and shiny, coaly patches. His black hair fell over his eyes, and his face was dark and dirty and sunken, so that at first I did not recognize him. There was a red cut across the lower part of his face.

"Stop!" he cried, when I was within ten yards of him, and I stopped. His voice was hoarse. "Where do you come from?" he said.

I thought, surveying him.

"I come from Mortlake," I said. "I was buried near the pit the Martians made about their cylinder. I have worked my way out and escaped."

"There is no food about here," he said. "This is my country. All this hill down to the river, and back to Clapham, and up to the edge of the common. There is only food for one. Which way are you going?"

I answered slowly.

"I don't know," I said. "I have been buried in the ruins of a house thirteen or fourteen days. I don't know what has happened."

He looked at me doubtfully, then started, and looked with a changed expression.

"I've no wish to stop about here," said I. "I think I shall go to Leatherhead, for my wife was there."

He shot out a pointing finger.

"It is you," said he — "the man from Woking. And you weren't killed at Weybridge?"

I recognized him at the same moment.

"You are the artilleryman who came into my garden."

"Good luck!" he said. "We are lucky ones! Fancy *you*!" He put out a hand, and I took it. "I crawled up a drain," he said. "But they

didn't kill everyone. And after they went away
I got off toward Walton across the fields. But
— it's not sixteen days altogether — and your
hair is gray." He looked over his shoulder suddenly. "Only a rook," he said. "One gets to
know that birds have shadows these days. This
is a bit open. Let us crawl under those bushes
and talk."

"Have you seen any Martians?" I said. "Since
I crawled out ——"

"They've gone away across London," he said.
"I guess they've got a bigger camp there. Of a
night, all over there, Hampstead way, the sky
is alive with their lights. It's like a great city,
and in the glare you can just see them moving. By daylight you can't. But nearer — I
haven't seen them —" (he counted on his fingers) "five days. Then I saw a couple across
Hammersmith way carrying something big.
And the night before last" — he stopped and
spoke impressively — "it was just a matter of
lights, but it was something up in the air. I
believe they've built a flying machine, and are
learning to fly."

I stopped on hands and knees, for we had
come to the bushes.

"Fly!"

"Yes," he said, "fly."

I went on into a little bower, and sat down.

"It is all over with humanity," I said. "If

they can do that they will simply go round the world."

He nodded.

"They will. But — it will relieve things over here a bit. And besides —" he looked at me — "aren't you satisfied it *is* up with humanity? I am. We're down; we're beat."

I stared. Strange as it may seem, I had not arrived at this fact — a fact perfectly obvious so soon as he spoke. I had still held a vague hope; rather, I had kept a lifelong habit of mind. He repeated his words, "we're beat." They carried absolute conviction.

"It's all over," he said. "They've lost *one* — just *one*. And they've made their footing good and crippled the greatest power in the world. They've walked over us. The death of that one at Weybridge was an accident. And these are only pioneers. They kept on coming. These green stars — I've seen none these five or six days, but I've no doubt, they're falling somewhere every night. Nothing's to be done. We're under! We're beat!"

I made him no answer. I sat staring before me, trying in vain to devise some countervailing thought.

"This isn't a war," said the artilleryman. "It never was a war, any more than there's war between men and ants."

Suddenly I recalled the night in the observatory.

"After the tenth shot they fired no more —
at least, until the first cylinder came."

"How do you know?" said the artilleryman.
I explained. He thought. "Something wrong
with the gun," he said. "But what if there is?
They'll get it right again. And even if there's
a delay, how can it alter the end? It's just men
and ants. There's the ants builds their cities,
live their lives, have wars, revolutions, until
the men want them out of the way, and then
they go out of the way. That's what we are
now — just ants. Only ——"

"Yes," I said.

"We're eatable ants."

We sat looking at each other.

"And what will they do with us?" I said.

"That's what I've been thinking," he said —
"that's what I've been thinking. After Weybridge I went south — thinking. I saw what
was up. Most of the people were hard at it
squealing and exciting themselves. But I'm not
so fond of squealing. I've been in sight of death
once or twice; I'm not an ornamental soldier,
and at the best and worst, death — it's just
death. And it's the man that keeps on thinking
comes through. I saw every one tracking away
south. Says I, 'Food won't last this way,' and
I turned right back. I went for the Martians
like a sparrow goes for man. All round" — he
waves a hand to the horizon — "they're starv-

ing in heaps, bolting, treading on each other.
. . ."

He saw my face, and halted awkwardly.

"No doubt lots who had money have gone
away to France," he said. He seemed to hesi-
tate whether to apologize, met my eyes, and
went on: "There's food all about here. Canned
things in shops; wines, spirits, mineral waters;
and the water mains in drains are empty. Well,
I was telling you what I was thinking. 'Here's
intelligent things,' I said, 'and it seems they
want us for food. First, they'll smash us up —
ships, machines, guns, cities, all the order and
organization. All that will go. If we were the
size of ants we might pull through. But we're
not. It's all too bulky to stop. That's the first
certainty.' Eh?"

I assented.

"It is; I've thought it out. Very well, then —
next; at present we're caught as we're wanted.
A Martian has only to go a few miles to get a
crowd on the run. And I saw one, one day, out
by Wandsworth, picking houses to pieces and
routing among the wreckage. But they won't
keep on doing that. So soon as they've settled
all our guns and ships, and smashed our railways, and done all the things they are doing
over there, they will begin catching us syste-
matic, picking the best and storing us in cages
and things. That's what they will start doing in

a bit. Lord! they haven't begun on us yet!
Don't you see that?"

"Not begun!" I exclaimed.

"Not begun. All that's happened so far is
through our not having the sense to keep quiet
— worrying them with guns and such foolery.
And losing our heads, and rushing off in crowds
to where there wasn't any more safety than
where we were. They don't want to bother
us yet. They're making their things — making
all the things they couldn't bring with them,
getting things ready for the rest of their people. Very likely that's why the cylinders have
stopped for a bit, for fear of hitting those who
are here. And instead of our rushing about
blind, on the howl, or getting dynamite on the
chance of busting them up, we've got to fix
ourselves up according to the new state of affairs. That's how I figure it out. It isn't quite
according to what a man wants for his species,
but it's about what the facts point to. And
that's the principle I acted upon. Cities, nations, civilization, progress — it's all over.
That game's up. We're beat."

"But if that is so, what is there to live for?"

The artilleryman looked at me for a moment.

"There won't be any more blessed concerts
for a million years or so; there won't be any
Royal Academy of Arts, and no nice little
feeds at restaurants. If it's amusement you're
after, I reckon the game is up. If you've got

any drawing-room manners or a dislike to eating peas with a knife or dropping aitches, you'd better chuck 'em away. They ain't no further use."

"You mean ——"

"I mean that men like me are going on living — for the sake of the breed. I tell you, I'm grim set on living. And if I'm not mistaken, you'll show what insides *you've* got, too, before long. We aren't going to be exterminated. And I don't mean to be caught either, and tamed and fattened and bred like a thundering ox. Ugh! Fancy those brown creepers!"

"You don't mean to say ——"

"I do. I'm going on. Under their feet. I've got it planned; I've thought it out. We men are beat. We don't know enough. We've got to learn before we've got a chance. And we've got to live and keep independent while we learn. See! That's what has to be done."

I stared, astonished, and stirred profoundly by the man's resolution.

"Great God!" cried I. "But you are a man indeed!" And suddenly I gripped his hand.

"Eh!" he said, with his eyes shining. "I've thought it out, eh?"

"Go on," I said.

"Well, those who mean to escape their catching must get ready. I'm getting ready. Mind you, it isn't all of us that are made for wild beasts; and that's what it's got to be. That's

why I watched you. I had my doubts. You're
slender. I didn't know that it was you, you
see, or just how you'd been buried. All these —
the sort of people that lived in these houses,
and all those damn little clerks that used to
live down that way — they'd be no good. They
haven't any spirit in them — no proud dreams
and no proud lusts; and a man who hasn't one
or the other — Lord! what is he but funk and
precautions? They just used to skedaddle off
to work — I've seen hundreds of 'em, bit of
breakfast in hand, running wild and shining
to catch their little season-ticket train, for
fear they'd get dismissed if they didn't; working at businesses they were afraid to take the
trouble to understand; skedaddling back for
fear they wouldn't be in time for dinner;
keeping indoors after dinner for fear of the
back streets, and sleeping with the wives they
married, not because they wanted them, but
because they had a bit of money that would
make for safety in their one little miserable
skedaddle through the world. Lives insured
and a bit invested for fear of accidents. And
on Sundays — fear of the hereafter. As if hell
was built for rabbits! Well, the Martians will
just be a godsend to these. Nice roomy cages,
fattening food, careful breeding, no worry.
After a week or so chasing about the fields
and lands on empty stomachs, they'll come and
be caught cheerful. They'll be quite glad after a

bit. They'll wonder what people did before there were Martians to take care of them. And the bar loafers, and mashers, and singers — I can imagine them. I can imagine them," he said, with a sort of somber gratification. "There'll be any amount of sentiment and religion loose among them. There's hundreds of things I saw with my eyes that I've only begun to see clearly these last few days. There's lots will take things as they are — fat and stupid; and lots will be worried by a sort of feeling that it's all wrong, and that they ought to be doing something. Now whenever things are so that a lot of people feel they ought to be doing something, the weak, and those who go weak with a lot of complicated thinking, always make for a sort of do-nothing religion, very pious and superior, and submit to persecution and the will of the Lord. Very likely you've seen the same thing. It's energy in a gale of funk, and turned clean inside out. These cages will be full of psalms and hymns and piety. And those of a less simple sort will work in a bit of — what is it? — eroticism."

He paused.

"Very likely these Martians will make pets of some of them; train them to do tricks — who knows? — get sentimental over the pet boy who grew up and had to be killed. And some, maybe, they will train to hunt us."

"No," I cried, "that's impossible! No human being ——"

"What's the good of going on with such lies?" said the artilleryman. "There's men who'd do it cheerful. What nonsense to pretend there isn't?"

And I succumbed to his conviction.

"If they come after me," he said — "Lord, if they come after me!" and subsided into a grim meditation.

I sat contemplating these things. I could find nothing to bring against this man's reasoning. In the days before the invasion no one would have questioned my intellectual superiority to his — I, a professed and recognized writer on philosophical themes, and he, a common soldier; and yet he had already formulated a situation that I had scarcely realized.

"What are you doing?" I said, presently. "What plans have you made?"

He hesitated.

"Well, it's like this," he said. "What have we to do? We have to invent a sort of life where man can live and breed, and be sufficiently secure to bring the children up. Yes— wait a bit, and I'll make it clearer what I think ought to be done. The tame ones will go like all tame beasts; in a few generations they'll be big, beautiful, rich-blooded, stupid — rubbish! The risk is that we who keep wild will go savage — degenerate into a sort of big savage rat. . . . You see, how I mean to live is underground. I've been thinking about the drains. Of course those who don't know drains think horrible things; but under this London are miles and miles — hundreds of miles — and a few days' rain and London empty will leave them sweet and clean. The main drains are big enough and airy enough for anyone. Then there's cellars, vaults, stores, from which bolting passages may be made to the drains. And the railway tunnels and subways. Eh? You begin to see? And we form a band — able-bodied, clean-minded men. We're not going to pick up any rubbish that drifts in. Weaklings go out again."

"As you meant me to go?"

"Well — I parleyed, didn't I?"

"We won't quarrel about that. Go on."

"Those who stop obey orders. Able-bodied, clean-minded women we want also — mothers and teachers. No lackadaisical ladies — no blasted rolling eyes. We can't have any weak or silly. Life is real again, and the useless and cumbersome and mischievous have to die. They ought to die. They ought to be willing to die. It's a sort of disloyalty, after all, to live and taint the race. And they can't be happy. Moreover, dying's none so dreadful; it's the funking makes it bad. And in all those places we shall gather. Our district will be London. And we may even be able to keep a watch, and run

about in the open when the Martians keep
away. Play cricket, perhaps. That's how we
shall save the race. Eh? It's a possible thing?
But saving the race is nothing in itself. As I
say, that's only being rats. It's saving our
knowledge and adding to it is the thing. There
men like you come in. There's books, there's
models. We must make great safe places down
deep, and get all the books we can; not novels
and poetry swipes, but ideas, science books.
That's where men like you come in. We must
go to the British Museum and pick all those
books through. Especially we must keep up
our science — learn more. We must watch these
Martians. Some of us must go as spies. When
it's all working, perhaps I will. Get caught, I
mean. And the great thing is, we must leave
the Martians alone. We mustn't even steal. If
we get in their way, we clear out. We must
show them we mean no harm. Yes, I know.
But they're intelligent things, and they won't
hunt us down if they have all they want, and
think we're just harmless vermin."

The artilleryman paused and laid down a
brown hand upon my arm.

"After all, it may not be so much we may
have to learn before — Just imagine this:
Four or five of their fighting-machines suddenly starting off — Heat Rays right and left,
and not a Martian in 'em. Not a Martian in
'em, but men — men who have learned the way

how. It may be in my time, even — those men. Fancy having one of them lovely things, with its Heat Ray wide and free! Fancy having it in control! What would it matter if you smashed to smithereens at the end of the run, after a bust like that? I reckon the Martians'll open their beautiful eyes! Can't you see them, man? Can't you see them hurrying, hurrying — puffing and blowing and hooting to their other mechanical affairs? Something out of gear in every case. And swish, bang, rattle, swish! just as they are fumbling over it, *swish* comes the Heat Ray, and, behold! man has come back to his own."

For a while the imaginative daring of the artilleryman, and the tone of assurance and courage he assumed, completely dominated my mind. I believed unhesitatingly both in his forecast of human destiny and in the practicability of his astonishing scheme, and the reader who thinks me susceptible and foolish must contrast his position, reading steadily with all his thoughts about his subject, and mine, crouching fearfully in the bushes and listening, distracted by apprehension. We talked in this manner through the early morning time, and later crept out of the bushes, and, after scanning the sky for Martians, hurried precipitately to the house on Putney Hill where he had made his lair. It was the coal cellar of the place, and when I saw the work

he had spent a week upon — it was a burrow
scarcely ten yards long, which he designed to
reach to the main drain on Putney Hill — I
had my first inkling of the gulf between his
dreams and his powers. Such a hole I could
have dug in a day. But I believed in him sufficiently to work with him all that morning
until past midday at his digging. We had a
garden barrow and shot the earth we removed against the kitchen range. We refreshed
ourselves with a tin of mock-turtle soup and
wine from the neighboring pantry. I found a
curious relief from the aching strangeness of
the world in this steady labor. As we worked, I
turned his project over in my mind, and presently objections and doubts began to arise;
but I worked there all the morning, so glad
was I to find myself with a purpose again.
After working an hour I began to speculate on
the distance one had to go before the cloaca
was reached, the chances we had of missing it
altogether. My immediate trouble was why we
should dig this long tunnel, when it was possible to get into the drain at once down one of
the manholes, and work back to the house. It
seemed to me, too, that the house was incon-
veniently chosen, and required a needless
length of tunnel. And just as I was beginning
to face these things, the artilleryman stopped
digging, and looked at me.

"We're working well," he said. He put down

his spade. "Let us knock off a bit," he said. "I think it's time we reconnoitered from the roof of the house."

I was for going on, and after a little hesitation, he resumed his spade; and then suddenly I was struck by a thought. I stopped, and so did he at once.

"Why were you walking about the Common," I said, "instead of being here?"

"Taking the air," he said. "I was coming back. It's safer by night."

"But the work?"

"Oh, one can't always work," he said, and in a flash I saw the man plain. He hesitated, holding his spade. "We ought to reconnoiter now," he said, "because if any come near they may hear the spades and drop upon us unawares."

I was no longer disposed to object. We went together to the roof and stood on a ladder peeping out of the roof door. No Martians were to be seen, and we ventured out on the tiles, and slipped down under shelter of the parapet.

From this position a shrubbery hid the greater portion of Putney, but we could see the river below, a bubbly mass of red weed, and the low parts of Lambeth flooded and red. The red creeper swarmed up the trees about the old palace, and their branches stretched gaunt and dead, and set with shriveled leaves,

from amid its clusters. It was strange how
entirely dependent both these things were
upon flowing water for their propagation.
About us neither had gained a footing; labur-
nums, pink mays, snowballs, and trees of ar-
borvitæ, rose out of laurels and hydrangeas,
green and brilliant into the sunlight. Beyond
Kensington dense smoke was rising, and that
and a blue haze hid the northward hills.

The artilleryman began to tell me of the
sort of people who still remained in London.

"One night last week," he said, "some fools
got the electric light in order, and there was
all Regent Street and the Circus ablaze,
crowded with painted and ragged drunkards,
men and women, dancing and shouting till
dawn. A man who was there told me. And as
the day came they became aware of a fighting
machine standing near by the Langham and
looking down at them. Heaven knows how long
he had been there. It must have given some of
them a nasty turn. He came down the road
toward them, and picked up nearly a hundred
too drunk or frightened to run away."

Grotesque gleam of a time no history will
ever fully describe!

From that, in answer to my questions, he
came round to his grandoise plans again. He
grew enthusiastic. He talked so eloquently of
the possibility of capturing a fighting machine
that I more than half believed in him again.

But now that I was beginning to understand something of his quality, I could divine the stress he laid on doing nothing precipitately. And I noted that now there was no question that he personally was to capture and fight the great machine.

After a time we went down to the cellar. Neither of us seemed disposed to resume digging, and when he suggested a meal, I was nothing loath. He became suddenly very generous, and when we had eaten he went away and returned with some excellent cigars. We lit these, and his optimism glowed. He was inclined to regard my coming as a great occasion.

"There's some champagne in the cellar," he said.

"We can dig better on this Thames-side burgundy," said I.

"No," said he; "I am host today. Champagne! Great God! we've a heavy enough task before us! Let us take a rest and gather strength while we may. Look at these blistered hands!"

And pursuant to this idea of a holiday, he insisted upon playing cards after we had eaten. He taught me euchre, and after dividing London between us, I taking the northern side and he the southern, we played for parish points. Grotesque and foolish as this will seem to the sober reader, it is absolutely true, and, what is more remarkable, I found the card game and several others we played extremely interesting.

Strange mind of man! that, with our species upon the edge of extermination or appalling degradation, with no clear prospect before us but the chance of a horrible death, we could sit following the chance of this painted pasteboard, and playing the "joker" with vivid delight. Afterward he taught me poker, and I beat him at three tough chess games. When dark came we decided to take the risk, and lit a lamp.

After an interminable string of games, we supped, and the artilleryman finished the champagne. We went on smoking the cigars. He was no longer the energetic regenerator of his species I had encountered in the morning. He was still optimistic, but it was a less kinetic, a more thoughtful optimism. I remember he wound up with my health, proposed in a speech of small variety and considerable intermittence. I took a cigar, and went upstairs to look at the lights of which he had spoken, that blazed so greenly along the Highgate hills.

At first I stared unintelligently across the London valley. The northern hills were shrouded in darkness; the fires near Kensington glowed redly, and now and then an orange-red tongue of flame flashed up and vanished in the deep blue night. All the rest of London was black. Then, nearer, I perceived a strange light, a pale, violet-purple fluorescent glow,

quivering under the night breeze. For a space
I could not understand it, and then I knew
that it must be the red weed from which this
faint irradiation proceeded. With that realization my dormant sense of wonder, my sense of
the proportion of things, awoke again. I
glanced from that to Mars, red and clear,
glowing high in the west, and then gazed long
and earnestly at the darkness of Hampstead
and Highgate.

I remained a very long time upon the roof,
wondering at the grotesque changes of the day.
I recalled my mental states from the midnight
prayer to the foolish card-playing. I had a
violent revulsion of feeling. I remember I flung
away the cigar with a certain wasteful symbo-
lism. My folly came to me with glaring exag-
geration. I seemed a traitor to my wife and to
my kind; I was filled with remorse. I resolved
to leave this strange undisciplined dreamer of
great things to his drink and gluttony, and to
go on into London. There, it seemed to me, I
had the best chance of learning what the Martians and my fellow men were doing. I was
still upon the roof when the late moon rose.

8. Dead London

AFTER I HAD PARTED from the artilleryman,
I went down the hill, and by the High Street
across the bridge to Fulham. The red weed
was tumultuous at that time, and nearly choked
the bridge roadway; but its fronds were already whitened in patches by the spreading
disease that presently removed it so swiftly.

At the corner of the lane that runs to Putney
Bridge station I found a man lying. He was as
black as a sweep with the black dust, alive, but
helplessly and speechlessly drunk. I could get
nothing from him but curses and furious
lunges at my head. I think I should have stayed
by him but for the brutal expression on his
face.

There was black dust along the roadway

from the bridge onward, and it grew thicker
in Fulham. The streets were horribly quiet. I
got food — sour, hard, and moldy, but quite
eatable — in a baker's shop here. Some way
toward Walham Green the streets became clear
of powder, and I passed a white terrace of
houses on fire; the noise of the burning was
an absolute relief. Going on toward Brompton,
the streets were quiet again.

Here I came once more upon the black powder in the streets and upon dead bodies. I saw
altogether about a dozen in the length of the
Fulham Road. They had been dead many days,
so that I hurried quickly past them. The black
powder covered them over, and softened their
outlines. One or two had been disturbed by
dogs.

Where there was no black powder, it was
curiously like a Sunday in the City, with the
closed shops, the houses locked up and the
blinds drawn, the desertion, and the stillness.
In some places plunderers had been at work,
but rarely at other than the provision and wine
shops. A jeweler's window had been broken
open in one place, but apparently the thief had
been disturbed, and a number of gold chains
and a watch lay scattered on the pavement. I
did not trouble to touch them. Farther on was
a tattered woman in a heap on a doorstep; the
hand that hung over her knee was gashed and

bled down her rusty brown dress, and a smashed magnum of champagne formed a pool across the pavement. She seemed asleep, but she was dead.

The farther I penetrated into London, the profounder grew the stillness. But it was not so much the stillness of death — it was the stillness of suspense, of expectation. At any time the destruction that had already singed the northwestern borders of the metropolis, and had annihilated Ealing and Kilburn, might strike among these houses and leave them smoking ruins. It was a city condemned and derelict. . . .

In South Kensington the streets were clear of dead and of black powder. It was near South Kensington that I first heard the howling. It crept almost imperceptibly upon my senses. It was a sobbing alternation of two notes, "Ulla, ulla, ulla, ulla," keeping on perpetually. When I passed streets that ran northward it grew in volume, and houses and buildings seemed to deaden and cut it off again. It came in a full tide down Exhibition Road. I stopped, staring toward Kensington Gardens, wondering at this strange, remote wailing. It was as if that mighty desert of houses had found a voice for its fear and solitude.

"Ulla, ulla, ulla, ulla," wailed that super-human note — great waves of sound sweeping

down the broad, sunlit roadway, between the
tall buildings on each side. I turned northward,
marveling, toward the iron gates of Hyde
Park. I had half a mind to break into the
Natural History Museum and find my way up
to the summits of the towers, in order to see
across the park. But I decided to keep to the
ground, where quick hiding was possible, and
so went up on the Exhibition Road. All the
large mansions on each side of the road were
empty and still, and my footsteps echoed
against the sides of the houses. At the top,
near the park gate, I came upon a strange
sight — a bus overturned, and the skeleton of
a horse picked clean. I puzzled over this for a
time, and then went on to the bridge over the
Serpentine. The voice grew stronger and
stronger, though I could see nothing above
the housetops on the north side of the park,
save a haze of smoke to the northwest.

"Ulla, ulla, ulla, ulla," cried the voice, coming, as it seemed to me, from the district about
Regent's Park. The desolating cry worked
upon my mind. The mood that had sustained
me passed. The wailing took possession of me.
I found I was intensely weary, footsore, and
now again hungry and thirsty.

It was already past noon. Why was I wandering alone in this city of the dead? Why was I
alone when all London was lying in state, and

in its black shroud? I felt intolerably lonely.
My mind ran on old friends that I had forgot-
ten for years. I thought of the poisons in the
chemists' shops, of the liquors the wine mer-
chants stored; I recalled the two sodden creatures of despair, who so far as I knew, shared
the city with myself. . . .

I came into Oxford Street by the Marble
Arch, and here again were black powder and
several bodies, and an evil, ominous smell from
the gratings of the cellars of some of the
houses. I grew very thirsty after the heat of
my long walk. With infinite trouble I managed
to break into a public house and get food and
drink. I was weary after eating, and went into
the parlor behind the bar, and slept on a black
horsechair sofa I found there.

I awoke to find that dismal howling still in
my ears, "Ulla, ulla, ulla, ulla." It was now
dusk, and after I had routed out some biscuits
and a cheese in the bar — there was a meat
safe, but it contained nothing but maggots —
I wandered on through the silent residential
squares to Baker Street — Portman Square is
the only one I can name — and so came out at
last upon Regent's Park. And as I emerged
from the top of Baker Street, I saw far away
over the trees in the clearness of the sunset
the hood of the Martian giant from which this
howling proceeded. I was not terrified. I came

upon him, as if it were a matter of course. I
watched him for some time, but he did not
move. He appeared to be standing and yelling,
for no reason that I could discover.

I tried to formulate a plan of action. That
perpetual sound of "Ulla, ulla, ulla, ulla," confused my mind. Perhaps I was too tired to be
very fearful. Certainly I was more curious to
know the reason of this monotonous crying
than afraid. I turned back away from the park
and struck into Park Road, intending to skirt
the park, went along under the shelter of the
terraces, and got a view of this stationary,
howling Martian from the direction of St.
John's Wood. A couple of hundred yards out of
Baker Street I heard a yelping chorus, and saw,
first a dog with a piece of putrescent red meat
in his jaws coming headlong toward me, and
then a pack of starving mongrels in pursuit of
him. He made a wide curve to avoid me, as
though he feared I might prove a fresh competitor. As the yelping died away down the silent
road, the wailing sound of "Ulla, ulla, ulla,
ulla," reasserted itself.

I came upon the wrecked handling machine
halfway to St. John's Wood station. At first I
thought a house had fallen across the road. It
was only as I clambered among the ruins that
I saw, with a start, this mechanical Samson
lying, with its tentacles bent and smashed and

twisted, among the ruins it had made. The forepart was shattered. It seemed as if it had driven blindly straight at the house, and had been overwhelmed in its overthrow. It seemed to me then that this might have happened by a handling machine escaping from the guidance of its Martian. I could not clamber among the ruins to see it, and the twilight was now so far advanced that the blood with which its seat was smeared, and the gnawed gristle of the Martian that the dogs had left, were invisible to me.

Wondering still more at all that I had seen, I pushed on toward Primrose Hill. Far away, through a gap in the trees, I saw a second Martian, as motionless as the first, standing in the park toward the Zoological Gardens, and silent. A little beyond the ruins about the smashed handling machine I came upon the red weed again, and found the Regent's Canal, a spongy mass of dark-red vegetation.

As I crossed the bridge, the sound of "Ulla, ulla, ulla, ulla," ceased. It was, as it were, cut off. The silence came like a thunderclap.

The dusky houses about me stood faint and tall and dim; the trees toward the park were growing black. All about me the red weed clambered among the ruins, writhing to get above me in the dimness. Night, the mother of fear and mystery, was coming upon me. But while that voice sounded the solitude, the desolation, had been endurable; by virtue of it London had still seemed alive, and the sense of life about me had upheld me. Then suddenly a change, the passing of something — I knew not what — and then a stillness that could be felt. Nothing but this gaunt quiet.

London about me gazed at me spectrally. The windows in the white houses were like the eye sockets of skulls. About me my imagination found a thousand noiseless enemies moving. Terror seized me, a horror of my temerity. In front of me the road became pitchy black as though it was tarred, and I saw a contorted shape lying across the pathway. I could not bring myself to go on. I turned down St. John's Wood Road, and ran headlong from this unendurable stillness toward Kilburn. I hid from the night and the silence, until long after midnight, in a cabmen's shelter in Harrow Road. But before the dawn my courage returned, and while the stars were still in the sky I turned once more toward Regent's Park. I missed my way among the streets, and presently saw down a long avenue, in the half-light of the early dawn, the curve of Primrose Hill. On the summit, towering up to the fading stars, was a third Martian, erect and motionless like the others.

An insane resolve possessed me. I would die

and end it. And I would save myself even the
trouble of killing myself. I marched on reck-
lessly toward this Titan, and then, as I drew
nearer and the light grew, I saw that a multitude of black birds was circling and clustering
about the hood. At that my heart gave a bound,
and I began running along the road.

I hurried through the red weed that choked
St. Edmund's Terrace (I waded breast-high
across a torrent of water that was rushing
down from the waterworks toward the Albert
Road), and emerged upon the grass before the
rising of the sun. Great mounds had been
heaped about the crest of the hill, making a
huge redoubt of it — it was the final and larg-
est place the Martians had made — and from
behind these heaps there rose a thin smoke
against the sky. Against the skyline an eager
dog ran and disappeared. The thought that
had flashed into my mind grew real, grew
credible. I felt no fear, only a wild, trembling
exultation, as I ran up the hill toward the
motionless monster. Out of the hood hung
lank shreds of brown, at which the hungry
birds pecked and tore.

In another moment I had scrambled up the
earthen rampart and stood upon its crest, and
the interior of the redoubt was below me. A
mighty space it was, with gigantic machines
here and there within it, huge mounds of ma-

terial and strange shelter places. And scattered
about it, some in their overturned war machines, some in the now rigid handling machines, and a dozen of them stark and silent
and laid in a row, were the Martians — *dead!*
— slain by the putrefactive and disease bacteria against which their systems were unpre-
pared; slain as the red weed was being slain;
slain, after all man's devices had failed, by
the humblest thing that God, in his wisdom,
had put upon this earth.

For so it had come about, as indeed I and
many men might have foreseen had not terror
and disaster blinded our minds. These germs
of disease have taken toll of humanity since
the beginning of things — taken toll of our
prehuman ancestors since life began here. But
by virtue of this natural selection of our kind
we have developed resisting power; to no
germs do we succumb without a struggle, and
to many — those that cause putrefaction in
dead matter, for instance — our living frames
are altogether immune. But there are no bacteria on Mars, and directly these invaders
arrived, directly they drank and fed, our
microscopic allies began to work their overthrow. Already when I watched them they
were irrevocably doomed, dying and rotting
even as they went to and fro. It was inevitable.
By the toll of a billion deaths man has bought

his birthright of the earth, and it is his against all comers; it would still be his were the Martians ten times as mighty as they are. For neither do men live nor die in vain.

Here and there they were scattered, nearly fifty altogether, in that great gulf they had made, overtaken by a death that must have seemed to them as incomprehensible as any death could be. To me also at that time this death was incomprehensible. All I knew was that these things that had been alive and so terrible to men were dead. For a moment I believed that the destruction of Sennacherib had been reported, that God had repented, that the Angel of Death had slain them in the night.

I stood staring into the pit, and my heart lightened gloriously, even as the rising sun struck the world to fire about me with his rays. The pit was still in darkness; the mighty engines, so great and wonderful in their power and complexity, so unearthly in their tortuous forms, rose weird and vague and strange out of the shadows toward the light. A multitude of dogs, I could hear, fought over the bodies that lay darkly in the depth of the pit, far below me. Across the pit on its farther lip, flat and vast and strange, lay the great flying machine with which they had been experimenting upon our denser atmosphere when decay and death arrested them. Death had come not a day too soon. At the sound of a cawing overhead I looked up at the huge fighting machine that would fight no more forever, at the tattered red shreds of flesh that dripped down upon the overturned seats on the summit of Primrose Hill.

I turned and looked down at the slope of the hill to where, enhaloed now in birds, stood those other two Martians that I had seen overnight, just as death had overtaken them. The one had died, even as it had been crying to its companions; perhaps it was the last to die, and its voice had gone on perpetually until the force of its machinery was exhausted. They glittered now, harmless tripod towers of shining metal, in the brightness of the rising sun.

All about the pit, and saved as by a miracle from everlasting destruction, stretched the great Mother of Cities. Those who have only seen London veiled in her somber robes of smoke can scarcely imagine the naked clearness and beauty of the silent wilderness of houses.

Eastward, over the blackened ruins of the Albert Terrace and the splintered spire of the Church, the sun blazed dazzling in a clear sky, and here and there some facet in the great wilderness of roofs caught the light and glared with a white intensity.

Northward were Kilburn and Hampstead, blue and crowded with houses; westward the great city was dimmed; and southward, beyond the Martians, the green waves of Regent's Park, the Langham Hotel, the dome of the Albert Hall, the Imperial Institute, and the giant mansions of the Brompton Road came out clear and little in the sunrise, the jagged ruins of Westminster rising hazily beyond. Far away and blue were the Surrey Hills, and the towers of the Crystal Palace glittered like two silver rods. The dome of St. Paul's was dark against the sunrise, and injured, I saw for the first time, by a huge gaping cavity on its western side.

And as I looked at this wide expanse of houses and factories and churches, silent and abandoned; as I thought of the multitudinous hopes and efforts, the innumerable hosts of lives that had gone to build this human reef, and of the swift and ruthless destruction that had hung over it all; when I realized that the shadow had been rolled back, and that men might still live in the streets, and this dear vast dead city of mine be once more alive and powerful, I felt a wave of emotion that was near akin to tears.

The torment was over. Even that day the healing would begin. The survivors of the people scattered over the country — leaderless, lawless, foodless, like sheep without a shepherd — the thousands who had fled by sea, would begin to return; the pulse of life, growing stronger and stronger, would beat again in the empty streets and pour across the vacant squares. Whatever destruction was done, the hand of the destroyer was stayed. All the gaunt wrecks, the blackened skeletons of houses that stared so dismally at the sunlit grass of the hill, would presently be echoing with the hammers of the restorers and ringing with the tapping of their trowels. At the thought I extended my hands toward the sky and began thanking God. In a year, thought I — in a year. . . .

With overwhelming force came the thought of myself, of my wife, and the old life of hope and tender helpfulness that had ceased forever.

9. Wreckage

And now comes the strangest thing in my story. Yet, perhaps, it is not altogether strange. I remember, clearly and coldly and vividly, all that I did that day until the time that I stood weeping and praising God upon the summit of Primrose Hill. And then I forgot.

Of the next three days I know nothing. I have learned since that, so far from my being the first discoverer of the Martian overthrow, several such wanderers as myself had already discovered this on the previous night. One man — the first — had gone to St. Martin's-le-Grand, and, while I sheltered in the cabmen's hut, had contrived to telegraph to Paris. Thence the joyful news had flashed all over the world; a thousand cities, chilled by ghastly apprehensions, suddenly flashed into frantic illuminations; they knew of it in Dublin, Edinburgh, Manchester, Birmingham, at the time when I stood upon the verge of the pit. Already men, weeping with joy, as I have heard, shouting and staying their work to shake hands and shout, were making up trains, even as near as Crewe, to descend upon London. The church bells that had ceased a fortnight since suddenly caught the news, until all England was bell-ringing. Men on cycles, lean-faced, unkempt, scorched along every country lane shouted of unhoped deliverance, shouting to gaunt, staring figures of despair. And for the food! Across the Channel, across the Irish Sea, across the Atlantic, corn, bread, and meat were tearing to our relief. All the shipping in the world seemed going Londonward in those days. But of all this I have no memory. I drifted — a demented man. I found myself in a house of kindly people, who had found me on the third day wandering, weeping, and raving through the streets of St. John's Wood. They have told me since that I was singing some inane doggerel about "The Last Man Left Alive! Hurrah! The Last Man Left Alive!" Troubled as they were with their own affairs, these people, whose names, much as I would like to express my gratitude to them, I may not even give here, nevertheless cumbered themselves with me, sheltered me, and protected me from myself. Apparently they had learned something of my story from me during the days of my lapse.

Very gently, when my mind was assured again, did they break to me what they had learned of the fate of Leatherhead. Two days after I was imprisoned it had been destroyed, with every soul in it, by a Martian. He had swept it out of existence, as it seemed, without any provocation, as a boy might crush an ant hill, in a mere wantonness of power.

I was a lonely man, and they were very kind to me. I was a lonely man and a sad one, and they bore with me. I remained with them four days after my recovery. All that time I felt a vague, a growing craving to look once more on whatever remained of the little life that seemed so happy and bright in my past. It was a mere hopeless desire to feast upon my misery. They dissuaded me. They did all they could to divert me from this morbidity. But at last I could resist the impulse no longer, and, promising faithfully to return to them, and parting, as I will confess, from these four-day friends with tears, I went out again into the streets that had lately been so dark and strange and empty.

Already they were busy with returning people; in places even there were shops open, and

I saw a drinking-fountain running water.

I remember how mockingly bright the day seemed as I went back on my melancholy pilgrimage to the little house at Woking, how busy the streets and vivid the moving life about me. So many people were abroad everywhere, busied in a thousand activities, that it seemed incredible that any great proportion of the population could have been slain. But then I noticed how yellow were the skins of the people I met, how shaggy the hair of the men, how large and bright their eyes, and that every other man still wore his dirty rags. Their faces seemed all with one of two expressions — a leaping exultation and energy or a grim resolution. Save for the expression of the faces, London seemed a city of tramps. The vestries were indiscriminately distributing bread sent us by the French government. The ribs of the few horses showed dismally. Haggard special constables with white badges stood at the corners of every street. I saw little of the mischief wrought by the Martians until I reached Wellington Street, and there I saw the red weed clambering over the buttresses of Waterloo Bridge.

At the corner of the bridge, too, I saw one of the common contrasts of that grotesque time — a sheet of paper flaunting against a thicket of the red weed, transfixed by a stick

that kept it in place. It was the placard of the
first newspaper to resume publication — the
Daily Mail. I bought a copy for a blackened
shilling I found in my pocket. Most of it was
in blank, but the solitary compositor who did
the thing had amused himself by making a
grotesque scheme of advertisement stereo on
the back page. The matter he printed was
emotional; the news organization had not as
yet found its way back. I learned nothing
fresh except that already in one week the examination of the Martian mechanisms had
yielded astonishing results. Among other
things, the article assured me what I did not
believe at the time, that the "Secret of Flying"
was discovered. At Waterloo I found the free
trains that were taking people to their homes.
The first rush was already over. There were few
people in the train, and I was in no mood for
casual conversation. I got a compartment to
myself, and sat with folded arms, looking
grayly at the sunlit devastation that flowed
past the windows. And just outside the terminus the train jolted over temporary rails, and
on either side of the railway the houses were
blackened ruins. To Clapham Junction the
face of London was grimy with powder of the
Black Smoke, in spite of two days of thunder-
storms and rain, and at Clapham Junction the
line had been wrecked again; there were hun-

dreds of out-of-work clerks and shopmen working side by side with the customary navvies,
and we were jolted over a hasty relaying.

All down the line from there the aspect of
the country was gaunt and unfamiliar; Wimbledon particularly had suffered. Walton, by
virtue of its unburned pine woods, seemed the
least hurt of any place along the line. The
Wandle, the Mole, every little stream, was a
heaped mass of red weed, in appearance between butcher's meat and pickled cabbage. The
Surrey pine woods were too dry, however, for
the festoons of the red climber. Beyond Wimbledon, within sight of the line, in certain
nursery grounds, were the heaped masses of
earth about the sixth cylinder. A number of
people were standing about it, and some sappers were busy in the midst of it. Over it
flaunted a Union Jack, flapping cheerfully in
the morning breeze. The nursery grounds were
everywhere crimson with the weed, a wide expanse of vivid color cut with purple shadows,
and very painful to the eye. One's gaze went
with infinite relief from the scorched grays and
sullen reds of the foreground to the blue-green
softness of the eastward hills.

The line on the London side of Woking station was still undergoing repair, so I descended
at Byfleet station and took the road to Maybury, past the place where I and the artillery-

man had talked to the hussars, and on by the spot where the Martian had appeared to me in the thunderstorm. Here, moved by curiosity, I turned aside to find, among a tangle of red fronds, the warped and broken dogcart, with the whitened bones of the horse scattered and gnawed. For a time I stood regarding these vestiges. . . .

Then I returned through the pine wood, neck-high with red weed here and there, to find the landlord of the Spotted Dog had already found burial, and so came home past the College Arms. A man standing at an open cottage door greeted me by name as I passed.

I looked at my house with a quick flash of hope that faded immediately. The door had been forced; it was unfastened, and was opening slowly as I approached.

It slammed again. The curtains of my study fluttered out of the open window from which I and the artilleryman had watched the dawn. No one had closed it since. The smashed bushes were just as I had left them nearly four weeks ago. I stumbled into the hall, and the house felt empty. The stair carpet was ruffled and discolored where I had crouched, soaked to the skin from the thunderstorm the night of the catastrophe. Our muddy footsteps I saw still went up the stairs.

I followed them to my study, and found ly-

ing on my writing table still, with the selenite
paperweight upon it, the sheet of work I had
left on the afternoon of the opening of the
cylinder. For a space I stood reading over my
abandoned arguments. It was a paper on the
probable development of Moral Ideas with the
development of the civilizing process; and the
last sentence was the opening of a prophecy:
"In about two hundred years," I had written,
"we may expect—" The sentence ended
abruptly. I remembered my inability to fix my
mind that morning, scarcely a month gone by,
and how I had broken off to get my *Daily
Chronicle* from the newsboy. I remembered
how I went down to the garden gate as he came
along, and how I had listened to his odd story
of "Men from Mars."

I came down and went into the dining room.
There was the mutton and bread, both far
gone now in decay, and a beer bottle overturned,
just as I and the artilleryman had left them.
My home was desolate. I perceived the folly of
the faint hope I had cherished so long. And
then a strange thing occurred. "It is no use,"
said a voice. "The house is deserted. No one
has been here these ten days. Do not stay here
to torment yourself. No one escaped but you."

I was startled. Had I spoken my thought
aloud? I turned, and the French window was

open behind me. I made a step to it, and stood looking out.

And there, amazed and afraid, even as I stood amazed and afraid, were my cousin and my wife — my wife white and tearless. She gave a faint cry.

"I came," she said. "I knew — knew ——"

She put her hand to her throat — swayed. I made a step forward, and caught her in my arms.

10. The Epilogue

I CANNOT BUT REGRET, now that I am concluding my story, how little I am able to contribute to the discussion of the many debatable questions which are still unsettled. In one respect I shall certainly provoke criticism. My particular province is speculative philosophy. My knowledge of comparative physiology is confined to a book or two, but it seems to me that Carver's suggestions as to the reason of the rapid death of the Martians is so probable as to be regarded almost as a proven conclusion. I have assumed that in the body of my narrative.

At any rate, in all the bodies of the Martians that were examined after the war, no bacteria except those already known as terrestrial species were found. That they did not bury any of

their dead, and the reckless slaughter they
perpetrated, point also to an entire ignorance
of the putrefactive process. But probable as
this seems, it is by no means a proven conclusion.

Neither is the composition of the Black
Smoke known, which the Martians used with
such deadly effect, and the generator of the
Heat Rays remains a puzzle. The terrible di-
sasters at the Ealing and South Kensington
laboratories have disinclined analysts for further investigations upon the latter. Spectrum
analysis of the black powder points unmis-
takably to the presence of an unknown element
with a brilliant group of three lines in the
green, and it is possible that it combines with
argon to form a compound which acts at once
with deadly effect upon some constitutent in
the blood. But such unproven speculations will
scarcely be of interest to the general reader,
to whom this story is addressed. None of the
brown scum that drifted down the Thames after
the destruction of Shepperton was examined at
the time, and now none is forthcoming.

The results of an anatomical examination
of the Martians, so far as the prowling dogs
have left such an examination possible, I have
already given. But everyone is familiar with
the magnificent and almost complete specimen
in spirits at the Natural History Museum, and

the countless drawings that have been made from it; and beyond that the interest of their physiology and structure is purely scientific.

A question of graver and universal interest is the possibility of another attack from the Martians. I do not think that nearly enough attention is being given to this aspect of the matter. At present the planet Mars is in conjunction, but with every return to opposition I, for one, anticipate a renewal of their adventure. In any case, we should be prepared. It seems to me that it should be possible to define the position of the gun from which the shots are discharged, to keep a sustained watch upon this part of the planet, and to anticipate the arrival of the next attack.

In that case the cylinder might be destroyed with dynamite or artillery before it was sufficiently cool for the Martians to emerge, or they might be butchered by means of guns so soon as the screw opened. It seems to me that they have lost a vast advantage in the failure of their first surprise. Possibly they see it in the same light.

Lessing has advanced excellent reasons for supposing that the Martians have actually succeeded in effecting a landing on the planet Venus. Seven months ago now, Venus and Mars were in alignment with the sun; that is to say, Mars was in opposition from the point of view

of an observer on Venus. Subsequently a
peculiar luminous and sinuous marking appeared on the unillumined half of the inner
planet, and almost simultaneously a faint dark
mark of a similar sinuous character was de-
tected upon a photograph of the Martian disk.
One needs to see the drawings of these appearances in order to appreciate fully their
remarkable resemblance in character.

At any rate, whether we expect another invasion or not, our views of the human future
must be greatly modified by these events. We
have learned now that we cannot regard this
planet as being fenced in and a secure abiding-
place for Man; we can never anticipate the
unseen good or evil that may come upon us suddenly out of space. It may be that in the larger
design of the universe this invasion from Mars
is not without its ultimate benefit for men; it
has robbed us of that serene confidence in
the future which is the most fruitful source of
decadence, the gifts to human science it has
brought are enormous, and it has done much
to promote the conception of the commonweal
of mankind. It may be that across the immensity of space the Martians have watched
the fate of these pioneers of theirs and learned
their lesson, and that on the planet Venus they
have found a securer settlement. Be that as it

may, for many years yet there will certainly
be no relaxation of the eager scrutiny of the
Martian disk, and those fiery darts of the sky,
the shooting stars, will bring with them as
they fall an unavoidable apprehension to all
the sons of men.

The broadening of men's views that has re-
sulted can scarcely be exaggerated. Before the
cylinder fell there was a general persuasion
that through all the deep of space no life existed beyond the petty surface of our minute
sphere. Now we see further. If the Martians
can reach Venus, there is no reason to suppose
that the thing is impossible for men, and when
the slow cooling of the sun makes this earth
uninhabitable, as at last it must do, it may
be that the thread of life that has begun here
will have streamed out and caught our sister
planet within its toils.

Dim and wonderful is the vision I have con-
jured up in my mind of life spreading slowly
from this little seedbed of the solar system
throughout the inanimate vastness of sidereal
space. But that is a remote dream. It may be,
on the other hand, that the destruction of the
Martians is only a reprieve. To them, and not
to us, perhaps, is the future ordained.

I must confess the stress and danger of the
time have left an abiding sense of doubt and

insecurity in my mind. I sit in my study writing by lamplight, and suddenly I see again the healing valley below set with writhing flames, and feel the house behind and about me empty and desolate. I go out into the Byfleet Road, and vehicles pass me, a butcher boy in a cart, a cabful of visitors, a workman on a bicycle, children going to school, and suddenly they become vague and unreal, and I hurry again with the artilleryman through the hot, brooding silence. Of a night I see the black powder darkening the silent streets, and the contorted bodies shrouded in that layer; they rise upon me tattered and dog-bitten. They gibber and grow fiercer, paler, uglier, mad distortions of humanity at last, and I wake, cold and wretched, in the darkness of the night.

I go to London and see the busy multitudes in Fleet Street and the Strand, and it comes across my mind that they are but the ghosts of the past, haunting the streets that I have seen silent and wretched, going to and fro, phantasms in a dead city, the mockery of life in a galvanized body. And strange, too, it is to stand on Primrose Hill, as I did but a day before writing this last chapter, to see the great province of houses, dim and blue through the haze of the smoke and mist, vanishing at last into the vague lower sky, to see the people walking to and fro among the flowerbeds on the hill, to see the sightseers about the Martian machine that stands there still, to hear the tumult of playing children, and to recall the time when I saw it all bright and clear-cut, hard and silent, under the dawn of that last great day. . . .

And strangest of all is it to hold my wife's hand again, and to think that I have counted her, and that she has counted me, among the dead.

About the Author
HERBERT GEORGE WELLS

HERBERT GEORGE WELLS, novelist, journalist, sociologist, and historian, was born in Bromley, England, in 1866, the son of a professional cricketer. As a child, Wells stealthily pursued his love of books in the library at the estate where his mother served as a housekeeper. When his family encountered financial troubles, Wells was apprenticed to a draper. He earned a scholarship to study biology at the Normal School of Science in London but lost interest before obtaining a degree.

Wells's first novel, *The Time Machine*, published in 1895, was a popular and critical success. Many other beloved works of fiction and nonfiction followed, including *The War of the Worlds, The Invisible Man*, and *The Island of Dr. Moreau.*

Wells died in his sleep in London in 1946. The characters and stories he crafted continue to thrill readers, listeners, and moviegoers alike, more than a century after they were written.

About the Introduction Author
ORSON SCOTT CARD

ORSON SCOTT CARD is the award-winning author of more than sixty books in many different genres. He is best known for his science fiction novels, including *Ender's Game*, winner of the Hugo Award, the Nebula Award, and the Hamilton-Brackett Award, and *Speaker for the Dead*, winner of the Hugo Award, the Nebula Award, and the Locus Award.